BLOODLINE

STORY OF THE REBORN

C.P. MILLER

Copyright © 2023 C.P. Miller.

All rights reserved. No part of this book may be reproduced, stored, or transmitted by any means—whether auditory, graphic, mechanical, or electronic—without written permission of both publisher and author, except in the case of brief excerpts used in critical articles and reviews. Unauthorized reproduction of any part of this work is illegal and is punishable by law.

ISBN: 979-8-89031-216-7 (sc)
ISBN: 979-8-89031-217-4 (hc)
ISBN: 979-8-89031-218-1 (e)

Because of the dynamic nature of the Internet, any web addresses or links contained in this book may have changed since publication and may no longer be valid. The views expressed in this work are solely those of the author and do not necessarily reflect the views of the publisher, and the publisher hereby disclaims any responsibility for them.

One Galleria Blvd., Suite 1900, Metairie, LA 70001
1-888-421-2397

CONTENTS

Chapter 1	*Being Alone*	1
Chapter 2	*Keeping Secrets*	13
Chapter 3	*Off track but on Track*	25
Chapter 4	*Getting to Know the Story*	33
Chapter 5	*The Right Actions*	47
Chapter 6	*Getting in Gear*	53
Chapter 7	*Enemy of my enemy's*	61
Chapter 8	*Plan in Motion*	73
Chapter 9	*Keeping Up with Aperients*	89
Chapter 10	*Among Kings*	95
Chapter 11	*Loose ends*	109
Chapter 12	*The Primary Objective*	125

CHAPTER 1

BEING ALONE

The planet, Mars. Year. unknown. Once a plush vibrant world becoming ravished by a bloody war now inhabited by its victor's a now middle-aged population passed their prime consumed with profit, slave labor and their own self interest, The wolves. a race of men and women with wolflike features, sharp teeth, long nails on their hands and feet covered in thick luscious hair from head to toe; the sin-tar's, a race of men, with The upper half of their body appearing as a normal man's Torso, with the lower half resembling the full body of a horse; and the amazons, a race of women. A group that came together to fight a war against a very powerful enemy, now maintaining peace among themselves by forming the kingdom of Mars under the rule of a high council leading them to become more peaceful in nature. As years turned into decades the population Suddenly find's themselves being hunted by new a threat in the form of a animal they call the shadow beast. These menacing yellow eyed creature's reaching heights of six to nine feet tall, stalking around on short muscular legs attached to a huge husky frame, very long thin muscular front arms, a long snout and sharp jagged teeth and nails resembling fishing hooks. Walking on all fours able to walk on its back legs as well. Only using the shadows as a doorway during the night. Coming out after every 2190 hours when the sun goes down ending what is known as the sun cycle and the moon comes out for 2190 hours starting the moon cycle, Four cycles completing a year keeping track of the days in a 24.6 hour period, the beast's attack and abduct people from the kingdom. For years, they created lights that shone as bright as the sun and built electric fences on the outside of the kingdom to keep the beast out, but that was not enough for the high council, which made their scientists work year after year to create three weapons. Three living, thinking, and self-enhancing weapons made up of two males and a female from the blood of a race that was whipped out by the war, created to protect and serve with their life anyone they see as their family under any circumstance. Two of them were raised by the head of the council, the other by the head scientist of Mars whom they would see as their father or uncle. The oldest of them was named Dominique. He was given to the head of council. The second of the three was named Jamal and was given to the head scientist. Jade, the youngest of the group, was also given to the head of the council. Being the only children on the planet their main instruction was to be seen not heard. their daily routine consists of tutoring, daily endurance tests and physicals, finding enjoyment only in their playtime by training themselves and each other in the ways of all things combat, as well as experimenting with engineering and all the sciences of over twenty different planets, making them fierce warriors and thinkers. As the years go on, the two older boys become the kingdom protectors. The girl is still to young but trains with them, eager to become one herself. The three clones stand around a tree in the backyard of the castle under the bright sun completing another day of training.

Jade: Dom, you ever feel (she pauses looking around). Alone?

Dom: Of course, who else you've seen on this planet of relics that resembles or even speak to us other then commands. (looking into the sky while sharpening a blade) You could be amazon, (as he looks at Jade). Our mothers could have been amazons. We are neither wolves nor sin-tar's, and only females are amazons. So what does that make us?

Jamal: I think of it as being unique, (laying back on a tree branch with his back to the trunk and hands behind his head).

They could have saved us from being wiped out.

Dom: Or they could be the reason we are alone. And what they once didn't wan't they now need to protect them.

Jade: Why not just ask Father or the high council?

Dom: I never get a straight answer out of them. They just keep telling me the same thing: they discovered us here when they came to Mars after their home world was destroyed, in other words depleted. My duties are far too important for me to travel, and their books tell you nothing you wan't to know. I guess, I just have this feeling. And the way the council looks at us sometimes. Makes me think, they're not telling us something. But I'll find out.

A woman stands there waiting for them as they walk up to the castle.

Woman: It's time for your first meal and then off to start your day.

Jade: Will Father be joining us this morning?

Woman: No, young one, he is very busy all day today, now inside for your meal.

After their meal, the three of them sit in a large carriage pulled by a large tiger, on the way to drop Jade off at her tutoring session and take the boys to the kingdom's lab. On the way, Jade happens to look at Dominique looking out the carriage window. She could see that everything he was saying he believed. Then she looks at Jamal as he kicks back sleeping. The carriage stops in front of her school. The wolf driver opens the doors.

Driver: We are here young one.

She nods at Dominique as she leaves; he nods back.

Jade: Thank you Driver (as she gets out).

She walks to the inside as they move on to the lab. The carriage stops in front of the kingdom's lab, a large glass building at the end of the kingdom. The driver opens the door.

Driver: We are here.

Dominique taps Jamal to wake up, and they get out.

Dom: Thank you, Driver (then he fixes a blade on his belt before walking toward the lab).

Jamal: Yeah, thanks (as he gets out stretching following Dom).

When they get inside, they are met by Jamal's father, the head scientist for the kingdom of Mars, a tall wolf man in glasses and lab coat.

Jamal: Greetings Father.

Dom: Greetings. Uncle.

HS: Greetings boys.

Jamal: So what do you have for us today?

HS: It's an all-terrain motorbike with boosters, made from on of the universe's strongest metals, equipped with hand-to-hand weapon, and firearm holder's.

They walk up to a black steel bike with large wheels.

Dom: Nice! (nodding his head).

Jamal: Can we try them out?

HS: Yes, but first we have something to brief you on before you head out.

They walk into a room with a large monitor on the wall and a table. They all sit and look at the monitor. A map of the east side of the forest comes up.

HS: About a few days ago, we sent a ship out on a routine exploration. An hour ago, the ship came back, but it crashed a few miles away west from here in the forest. We can't reach them by radio, so you need to go see if they are okay and if they brought anything or anyone back with them.

As they get ready to go, Dominique sits on his bike thinking about what or who it can be on the ship. Jamal walks up from the gun rack while putting a gun on his belt, gets on his bike, and then looks at Dominique.

Jamal: You all right?

Dom: Yeah, I'm good, let's go.

They leave the kingdom's lab and head to the location of the ship riding along the edge of the forest. They talk to each other and the kingdom's lab through headsets in their helmets.

Jamal: So what are you doing later?

Dom: Not much, what do you have in mind?

Jamal: Maybe we can take the jets for a spin.

Dom: I'm in, plus you could use some practice. (With a smirk on his face).

As they ride along the edge of the forest, a voice comes from the dashboard of the bikes.

Bike: You are five hundred yards away from your destination.

Dominique pops a wheelie as he takes the lead; as they get closer, the voice comes back.

Bike: You are one hundred yards away from your destination, fifty yards and closing. ten yards.

They stop at a clear area along the edge of the forest.

Bike: You have reached your destination.

They get off and gear up in black leg, arm, and chest protection with guns and weapons, Dominique with a short sword on his back, blades on each side of his waist and a small hand gun in a leg holster. Jamal with a shotgun on his back and two handguns on the sides of his waist and two leg holsters on each leg carrying two large handguns. Dominique pulls up the map from his handheld tracker and locates a trail.

Dom: Well, let's get to work.

As they walk farther into the dark forest on the trail, they hear a sound coming from their side from the top of the trees. Then there is a snapping sound, something large falls from the trees. They move in to see what it is that fell. They walk up and see a black saber tooth tiger lying on the ground with its neck broke.

Jamal: It looks like we're about to get busy (checking the tiger with his foot).

Dom: So watch out, these guys aren't playing.

    They keep walking on the trail. They hear a loud thump behind them, they turn around fast. As soon as they do, a shadow beast jumps at them. Jamal pulls his handguns and shoots at the beast. Dominique starts to run around the beast as Jamal shoots it. Midway around the beast, another shadow beast comes out of a shadow and hits Dominique in the face while standing on its back legs making a deep cut across Dominique's face. The hit makes his body swing around. Dominique comes back around with a jab, and with the other hand, he stabs the beast in the chest, then drags the blade upward making the blade cut its eye in half slicing through the top of its head. He kicks it into a spot of sunlight which causes the beast to turn into a puff of smoke. Dominique continues running around the first beast. He gets to the back of the beast and jumps at it off a large rock landing with his blades stuck in the back of the beast. The beast yells, and Jamal gets a good shot on the beast and shoots it right in the mouth out the back of the head; blood sprays everywhere. Dominique and the beast fall, Dominique gets up after the fall, dusting himself off.

Dom: You okay (as he walks toward Jamal with blood running down his face)?

Jamal: Yeah. Are you all right?

Dom: I'll be fine. Let's get back to the kingdom so I can get this fixed. The forest is pretty heavy today with shadow beast, and we are the only civilization on Mars. We can keep looking later.

They get back to the kingdom's lab and debrief as Dominique gets his face bandaged.

HS: What happened?

Jamal: We were on the trail of the ship, got into it with two shadow beasts, and came back for Dom's wound.

The head scientist looks at Dominique sitting on a chair getting bandaged.

HS: We will try again later, (taking a deep breath). You can leave now.

Jamal walks to his house by the lab. Dominique gets back in the carriage and heads to pick up Jade. Dominique looks at the people in the kingdom and wonders if he was even a part of something or is he something his real people didn't want. But for as long as he could remember, they have been on Mars with these people that are and look nothing like him but he protect. He feels he has to or they will get rid of him too. Doing things like this every day, but something in him loves the fighting, so he keeps on doing it, getting stronger and smarter. They pull up to Jade's school, and she gets in, staring at Dominique's face.

Jade: Rough day?

Dom: Not really (he could tell she wanted to know). It was a shadow beast.

Jade: Did you get it (at the edge of her seat)?

Dom: With one slice.

Jade: I can't wait until I'm out there with you guys, It's gonna be so awesome (with a big smile on her face).

Dominique and Jade get to the castle and go inside their rooms. Dominique hits the bed and shuts his eyes. Jade gets started on her homework. Almost instantly Dominique hears a knock on the door.

Woman: It's meal time, boy.

Dom: Thank you.

Dominique walks into the dining room and sees Jade and his father, the head of the high council, sitting at the table. His father is a short and buff wolf man in a long robe. Dominique has a seat.

Dom: Greetings. Father.

HC: Greetings boy.

Jade: Greetings Dom.

Dom: Greetings young one. (In a playful sarcastic tone).

Jade puts her hand to her mouth trying to hide a smile.

HC: Young one, I heard you weren't very present today in your studies, your so close. However do you think of joining the boys if you do not take training serious?

Jade: Yes sir. (lowering her head in shame as she pick at the food on her plate).

The HC looks at Dominique.

HC: So what happen today?

Dom: Nothing.

HC: So nothing did that to you're face?

Dom: It was a shadow beast, it got me, but I got it worst.

HC: That's good to hear, one less of those things around, keep that up and I feel Mars will soon be a safe place.

CHAPTER 2

KEEPING SECRETS

As the sun cycle ends starting the moon cycle, Dominique and Jamal think of a way to get rid of the shadow beast once and for all. They came up with the idea to let a few of them in a part of the kingdom and capture the ones they don't kill for testing to find where they might dwell because the only things they know is that the beast hunt only at night because the sun is deadly to them, and they can be killed by weapons. Dominique request for an appearance to ask the permission ofced to proceed with the plan. The council all sit in the meeting room, a large room that leads to stairs. At the top of the stairs sits the high council, the council members consist of three wolves, two men, one woman, and two sin-tars. All dressed in long white robes.

CM, woman: We have to find out a way to get rid of the beast, once and for all, for the sake of our people here on Mars.

CM s: She is right (then he looks at the head of the council)! You told us that your creations would do that for us. There are only two and the girl is too young, you said.

HC: Calm down, the young one is ready to play her part.

Then an Amazon woman walks into the meeting room.

Woman: He is here to speak with the council.

HC: Send him in (waving his arm).

She walks out and Dominique walks in.

Dom: Greetings, council (then he bows). I have the plan to get rid of the beast for good.

CM s: So what is it (in a smug voice)?

Dominique stops himself from jumping at the sin-tar.

Dom: I would like to cut off a part of the kingdom and let some of the beast in so we can test and study them to better understand how they work and potentially find a nest.

CM s: What! That's crazy. What will you do if one were to get loose?

Dom: That will not happen with us.

HC: I will let you do your job, you haven't disappointed me. yet.

CM s: Fine, this better work, I would hate to be in your position if it does not, (looking at Dominique).

Dom: I bet my life on it (looking back at him with a smile imagining himself throwing one of his blades between the sin-tars eyes).

HC: Well, if that is all, go now.

Dominique bowes and then walks out meeting Jamal outside of the high council's meeting room, they walk down the hall to the back of the castle.

Jamal: So you get the go-ahead?

Dom: Yeah, it's all set up.

Jamal: He went for keeping one of them for testing?

Dom: He's not truthful, but he's wise, plus he knows it could help in the eradication of the beast.

Later that night, Dominique and Jade stand facing each other behind the castle in the yard ready to fight. Jade swings wildly, Dominique moves around as he blocks every punch. Dominique grabs her wrist, pulls her to him and then knees her on the side. Jade stumbles back, Dominique kicks at her, she turns sideways and gives him a hit on his side, making him stumble to the side. Jade felt like she punched a wall. Dominique gives a roundhouse. Jade leans back so she will not get hit and then swings at Dominique. He blocks and then pushes her, making her fall. Jade rolls back getting to her feet almost as soon as she fell. Dominique jumps at her, she kicks him on the side of the head, and his head jerks. Dominique trips her and she falls on her side but gets up fast. Impressed, he could see how far she has come as well as the look she had in her eyes. He could tell without a doubt she was also like him, so he stands down.

Dom: Very good. I think you're ready to run with us this moon.

Jade: Yes sir! (with a smile).

Dom: Welcome to the team.

The next night the team set the bait of animal blood and guts at the opening of the trap in the kingdom. Dominique kneels facing the opening while filling the ground. They are all dressed in black gear from neck to toe with forearm, lower leg, and chest armor, Dominique with two swords on his back, one short, one long, a blade on each side. A few feet away on one side of him stands Jamal carrying four handguns in waist and leg holsters with a shotgun on his back. On the other side of Dominique stands Jade with a bo staff in her hand and a handgun strapped to her hip. The team stands in only a small dim spotlight with the dark surrounding them. Dominique stands.

Dom: Get ready!

Jade: You got it! (twirling the staff around).

Jamal: Here we go!

They see a herd of beast running toward them. A small group of beast runs into the dark before a few dim lights along the top of the tall walls around them come on and the electric fence at the entrance shuts. Dominique pulls his short sword as he starts running at the beast. One of them comes from the side, Dominique swings upward cutting it from the hip to the shoulder across the body. It splits in two. Another beast jumps on top of Dominique from behind the falling pieces of beast before they hit the ground. Jamal pulls a handgun, sees the beast on top of Dominique and shoots the beast in the head and then tosses a grenade at a group of beast running at him. The grenade goes off and the beast go flying. Dominique pushes the dead beast off and stands. He sees Jade running toward three beasts, and before she gets to them she plants the staff in the ground in front of her, using the staff to catapult herself in the air toward the beast. She drop-kicks one of them, making it fall and then she trips another and with the staff smacks the last one across the face, breaking its neck. It flips landing on its back. Jade doesn't see a beast running up behind her, but before it could make it to her, Dominique runs up and tackles the beast in the air as it jumps at her, pinning it to a high point on the wall next to them with his sword and then just lets it hang there. Dominique jumps down, pulling his long sword before landing cutting a beast in half, walking over the body. Jade spins the staff around and blades come out at the ends, she swings the staff like a bat, cutting two beasts on their necks killing them. A beast jumps at her from behind, she gives it a roundhouse to the face breaking its jaw, it falls and then she stabs it in the chest. Jamal walks up to a group of beasts with a shotgun and shots one in the face, one runs at him, and he hits it in the face with the end of the shotgun. It falls and then he shoots it in the head as it tries to get up. He then puts away the shotgun. Jamal sees a beast running at him, so he runs towards the beast. They lock up. Jamal grabs its neck as it tries to bite him and throws it to the ground and then stomps on its head, killing it. He takes the shotgun from his back and shoots three beasts coming at him, killing them. Dominique runs at three beast and with three swings of his sword, all three of them fall dead. As Jade pulls her staff from the face of a beast, she sees a beast running at Jamal as he looks down reloading the shotgun. She runs along side it at the top of the wall as it runs at Jamal, she throws the staff hitting the beast in the head. It goes in one side and comes out the other as it slams into a wall, making it stick to the wall dead. With the entire group of beast dead or injured, the team regroups.

Dom: Give me a report.

Jade: We left two alive.

Dom: That was a good run. Okay, let's get to work.

The next sun cycle, the team takes a walk along the edge of the forest heading west until they get to a large rock. Dominique pushes a button on his belt, a hole opens up on the rock; they jump in. One by one, they slide down a tube into three chairs in a large underground lab that the guys secretly created when they first started protecting. The lights come on in the lab. It's a large room with a few doors around the lab. The chairs sit on the end of the room made up of a few tables, desks, and some lockers to keep the weapons and gear next to some stairs that lead outside at the edge of the forest. They get up, and Dominique walks into a room that has one of the beasts that they captured from the last moon strapped to a table. He puts some gloves and a face mask on, walks over to the beast, and he starts to cut a piece of its flesh from its arm, walks in another room, shuts the door, and stays there almost three days. When Dominique comes out, he brings with him a cage with a cover over it and sits it on a table. Jade and Jamal walk up to Dominique. He takes off the cover and then opens the cage. Out walks a small black puppy with glowing green eyes, a short thick tail, sharp teeth, and thick black hair on its body.

Jamal: What's that?

Dom: This is Shadow. He's what I've been working on.

Jade: He's adorable (as she pets him).

Dom: And the first of its kind, mixing the DNA of a saber tooth tiger with the shadow beast, I created him. As our scout, he should be able to help us find the location of the shadow beast's nest. He's not like them, he can stand sunlight. Now he must eat and do his job.

Dominique walks up the stairs and opens the door.

Dom: Shadow, hunt!

Shadow jumps off the table and up the stairs into the forest. The next day Dominique and Jamal go back to the site of the trail in the jets. They hover over a clear patch in the forest to land the jets. They check the area and then start the mission.

They grab some weapons and head back on the path found by the trackers. The trail takes them to a thick part of the forest. They see a smashed and charred ship. They look around and go in and find two dead wolves, a man and a woman, in the cockpit.

Moving to the back of the ship, they find two large cases that they take out the ship and try to open but can't.

Dom: I'm going to take one of them to our lab. Call the other one in. I want to see what they were looking for.

Jamal calls the lab to tell them about their finding.

They get in the jet's rise and hover. Jamal goes east to the kingdom's lab, and Dominique takes off west to their forest lab. Dominique hovers over the rock and pushes the button on his belt. A hole opens in the rock. Dominique drops the case out of the jet and into the hole, and then the hole shuts, and he takes off east. Dominique lands and enters the kingdom's lab to debrief with the head scientist.

HS: You boys did well. you can rest up.

As days go by, they spend them in their lab working on opening the case. Dominique walks into a room to see Jamal cutting the case with a saw.

Dom: How's it going?

Jamal: Not so well, I think it's made out of some kind of armor.

Dominique grabs the case, takes it into the next room, straps a bomb to it, and sits it in a large steel box on the wall. The bomb goes off but the case still remains shut. he picks up the case, and sees a small hole in the wall.

Dom: There is something back here.

He set another bomb and it brings the wall holding the steel box down. On the other side was an old abandoned lab. They walk out to a balcony that wraps around the top half of the lab. They could see doors, tables and old computers all over the place covered with cob weds, dust and ashes. The lab looked like it was hit with a bomb or set on fire. As they walk down the stairs to look around, the lights come on. Jamal sees a large cannon on a table, he walks over to it and picks it up. The table lights up and a voice comes out from a speaker on the wall

Lab: Weapon #120, the grenade cannon, able to fire up to two grenades at once, kill power level 6%.

Then he walks into a room that has weapons all over the walls.

Jamal: I guess we've acquired a new wing.

Dom: Whoever attempted to make waste of this lab did not do a very good job.

Dominique finds a file locker full of charred folders and starts looking around. He comes across a piece of paper stuck to the bottom of the locker that was labeled (Project Protect) and starts reading it.

Folder: Project Protect are four clones of the seven, a powerful group of warriors that belonged to a race that once in habited Mars. Three of the clones have reached the stage of mobility. We will now move the three to the learning stage, they are taking to the teachings of the program we have put them in, and their minds have grown faster than we had hoped. The oldest has taken the leadership role and at the age of seven has begun to train himself in hand-to-hand combat. We have taken them out of the lab and in homes for more test to see if they can interact and protect in a home setting. It seems the test phase has worked, we have given them all names to feel at home. P-2 will be called Dominique, P-3 Jamal and P-4 Jade. P-1 has brain function, but his body just will not yet reach the stage of mobility. We will just have to move on to placing the other's. This is my report on year 7 of Project Protect.

The report was by the head scientist of Mars. Dominique hits the locker and walks back up the stairs to their lab and slams the paper on a table. Jade and Jamal see him rush out and follow him, they walk up to Dominique. Jamal picks up the paper and reads it.

Jamal: Well, that simplifies things (as he gives the paper to Jade), so that's what we are (as if he found clarity in knowing)

Jade grabs the folder, reads it, then she puts it back down.

Dom: They must stay in the dark about what we've learned. I feel there is more to this story then what has just been revealed .

Jamal: I'm not gonna say anything.

Jade looks down at the folder dazed.

Dom: Jade.

She shakes her head to confirm, without saying a word.

CHAPTER 3

OFF TRACK BUT ON TRACK

It's been several months since the team have seen the report, bringing the sun cycle to an end. The team finds something else to keep themselves busy. They make a plan to take out the shadow beast where they live. Dominique stands in front of the council to go over the mission.

Dom: We will be gone for the next moon cycle. There should be nothing to worry about since we put up a stronger fence, so it should be enough to hold them off until we return.

HC: Very well, we will see you after you get the job done.

Dominique walks out, goes upstairs to his room, and locks the door. Then he walks up to a bookcase and puts his hand up to the side of it, the case slides open, he walks in a doorway, and goes down a set of long stairs, the case shuts behind him.

He walks beside a wall into a large clubhouse under the castle the council gave to them when they were children. Jade sits at a table by a long glass window looking in at Jamal shooting the cannon he's modifying to make it more powerful. Dominique walks up to the glass and taps it to gets Jamal's attention. He looks and they walk to another room where the two rooms meet, a room with a wall full of guns that Jamal has been working on.

Dom: So what have we got?

Jamal: We got a faster fire time, a larger clip holding up to four grenades, and a kill power level of 10%.

Dom: Good, get some rest. We leave at night fall.

As the sun falls, they load up some tools and gear for the mission in one of Jade's new motor carts she's been working on. A large four seater cart with no top, two wheels in the front with a large flatbed sitting on top of a large single wheel. They get in and head out into the forest. They ride for about two miles before Dominique looks at his electronic map to see that a large part of the map south of them is missing, Dominique gets Jade to stop.

Dom: Hey, look at this (giving the map to Jamal).

Jamal: What's wrong with this thing?

Dom: I don't know. It was like that when I looked at it just now.

Jamal: Let's check it out.

Dom: Well, we are ahead a few hours. We could keep on from there; let's go.

They get out and gear up, Jade looks around the flatbed of the cart.

Jade: What, no food?

Dom: We eat what we catch.

She looks at them and sees they are serious. She puts her pack on in anger. They grab some guns and head out into the forest. They walk in formation with their guns out. After walking for a few miles, they come across a large hole in the ground that scratched from side to side a few miles and was also far across. Dominique lights a glow stick from his pack. He tosses it down the hole. The light hits the bottom revealing a nest of very large black scorpions.

Dom: It's not that deep, but there is something down there and it would take too long to go around. We have to jump it.

Dominique takes a few steps back pulls out a rope with a hook on the end of it and then starts running toward the hole. As soon as he gets to the hole's edge, he jumps and tosses the hook at a tall tree. It grabs a hold of a thick branch, and he swings over the hole and lands on the other side, rolling on a knee with his gun out. Checking the area, he calls his team from a headset.

Dom: Clear (as he stands up).

Jade and Jamal follow behind him. They roll their ropes back up and get ready to keep moving.

Dom: this side is thicker. I'll lead, Jamal take the rear.

Jamal: Got it.

Dominique pulls a sword from his back and they continue moving on, Dominique swings his sword to cut a path through the thick bushes. After about a half hour of cutting, they find a clear area in the forest and set up camp for some rest. As Jade sets up the fire, Dominique walks up to her with a bowe and arrow.

Dom: You killed any food yet?

She looks up at him like he said something wrong. Dominique walks away from her grabbing a spray bottle from his belt and sprays it in the air. A few seconds later they hear a loud noise come from the sky, and then a large bird comes from behind a cloud and comes down toward them. Dominique points the bow at the bird as it gets closer. They see it's a bird with large wings that has long sharp nails on the ends, a fat body, long skinny legs with sharp talons, and a fat neck with a cobra-like head. It flies around to pick a target. Dominique lets go of the arrow. the airrow torpedoes toward the beast bird. It clips and rips off a large part of its wing. The beast tries to fly but falls to the ground fast. It hits the ground braking both legs. Jamal walks in front of it, and it snaps at him. Jamal moves around playing with the bird. Dominique walks up from the side with a long sword, jumps up, cutting off its head with one swing as he lands. He picks up the head and drags it to the fire. They cut it up, clean, and cook the meat, and they eat and talk until they are full. Jade and Jamal get some rest, Dominique stands guard. They sleep for a few hours and then pick up camp and head out under the bright moon. As they keep south, Dominique starts to feel a strong chill come over his body.

Dom: You feel that too?

Jade: Yeah, what is it?

Jamal: We're about to find out.

They walk out to a thin part of the forest and see a tall, smooth rock, they check the area around the rock then move in. Carved into the rock were large symbols forming a circle. They could feel that the source of what they felt was coming from the rock. They stand around the rock for a minute looking for ways to see what it contained. Dominique pulls out some explosives from his pack. Right before he sets the charge, two people rise from the ground around them and one from the top of the rock stand facing them. Their whole bodies are the same colors as the forest trees and ground; they have no eyes and have very sharp teeth; there are two men and one woman. The team stands back to back and gets ready to fight.

Jamal: They look like they are made out of Mars (putting on some gloves with spikes on the knuckles).

Dom: Let's see if they are as tough as they look (with a blade in each hand).

The man on top of the rock crouches.

Man: Who goes there?

Dom: My name is Dominique, lead protector for the kingdom of Mars.

Man: The kingdom of Mars, you do not belong here. Go back or face the keepers of the elements.

Dom: Elements. (under his breath). Then face you we shall.

Man: So be it.

The team drop their packs. Jade pulls two daggers,

Dom: Rip them apart.

Jade and Jamal: Yes sir!

Jade makes the first move and runs toward the woman. Jade swings, the woman turns sideways and grabs Jade's wrist. Jade tries to hit her with the other hand but gets tossed into a thick tree then hits the ground dropping her daggers. Jamal moves next at the man on the ground. Jamal jumps coming down with his fist pulled back. The man moves back, Jamal fist hits the ground and they look at each other. Jamal swings and hits him in the chest, the man falls back, and disappears into the ground. Jamal looks around the area, Dominique and the man on the rock just look at each other for a while. Then the man jumps off the rock at Dominique, Dominique moves to the side and then swings at him. The man blocks then swings at Dominique. Dominique blocks, they push off of each other. The man comes at Dominique, Dominique moves behind a thick tree, the man phases through the tree hitting Dominique in the face, Dominique stumbles back then quickly lunges swinging back, but before he could connect, the man phases back in the tree and Dominique cuts the tree deep. Jade gets up, as the woman stands in front of her, Jade uses the tree to catapult herself at the woman. She grabs her taking the woman to the ground. They both get to their feet; facing each other before the woman sinks into the ground. Jamal walks around some trees to find the man he was fighting. The man comes out of a tree next to Jamal and hits him on the side, Jamal stumbles to the side but kicks at the man connecting to the man's face. The man hits a tree and disappears. Dominique and the other man stand facing each other, the man swings at Dominique. Dominique grabs his wrist and tosses him into a tree, and he disappears. The team regroups and looks around checking the area.

Dom: There must be something in that rock.

Then in front of the rock, the three forest people rise. The team gets ready.

Dom: You back for more?

Man: We do not wish to fight you anymore. We think we have something to tell you.

The team walks up to them and stands a few feet away.

CHAPTER 4

GETTING TO KNOW THE STORY

Man: Greetings, my name is Drell, I am a Martian native to this planet and head keeper of the seven elements. What clan or race are you from?

Dom: To tell you the truth, we don't know.

Drell: Hum, I see. We would like to take you to our leader so he can tell us if you're who we think you are.

Dom: Sure.

The Martians stand around the team, and then the ground they all stand on slowly sinks. As they go deeper, they start to see a large kingdom that looked like it was also made out of Mars, with a lot of Martians of all ages all around the city. Behind the city was a large castle, they all walk through the city to get to the castle behind it. They get to the castle and go in; they stop in a big room with stairs that led to a door.

Drell: Stay here.

Drell walks up the stairs and goes in the door, as they stand around, the man Jamal was fighting just looks at him. Jamal looks back, and then the woman walks up to Jamal.

Woman: Don't mind him, that's Nor-rock, we've only herd story's about your kind around here. My name is Ten-ja.

Jamal: I'm Jamal; this is Jade and Dominique.

Minutes later, Drell walks out with an older-looking Martian dressed in a long brown robe with a long Mossy beard and a young-looking woman. They approach the team.

Old man: Welcome to my kingdom I am known as Emperor, when you get in a place of power, names are no longer important. I see you already met my son and the other element keepers, this is my daughter Na-vel

Na-vel: Welcome.

Dom: We are the protectors for the kingdom of Mars. My name is Dominique; this is Jamal and Jade. We were on our way to the shadow beast nest, then we saw a missing part on our map. That's how we found that rock.

M.E: The elements must have sensed you, that would explain the mess-up with your electronics.

Dom: And what are these elements that you all speak of?

M.E: I will tell you all you need to know after we eat, you are our guest. Let's sit as we talk.

They walk to a wall and it opens from the middle to a room, inside was a large table. They all walk in and sit down, some more Martians walk out of the doors in the room with large plates of food, they eat, giving the team a chance to talk to the emperor.

M.E: They called themselves Vampires, they were one of the most powerful but peaceful breed of people on Mars and beyond. Long ago, the vampire's leader discovered a source of power that lived deep in the core of Mars. The source granted him the honor of handpicking seven of the vampires to become the first to control the elements of Mars. They are Wind, Water, Lightning, Thunder, Electricity, and Raw Power. The vampire leader put together a small army of one hundred to compete. They came up with seven of the brightest minds and strongest warriors to contain an element. Our people became friends with the seven when they became tangled in a large war that wiped all of the vampires out, all but the seven. They told us about a race called the wolves that constantly attacked them over the powers. The seven were able to fight them off with no problem even after the wolves received help from the sin-tars until one day the wolves were able to get the vampires infected with a flesh-eating virus that was slowly killing them. The seven were immune because of their powers and kept the wolves at bay as their army became too sick to help fight the waves of enemies. And when the time was right, the wolves came in hard, the seven were able to flee and came to the forest where we helped them escape; they created the rock and hid their powers within it. They went into what would be their last fight. We don't know what happened to them after. That's all we know.

Dom: What are you doing with the elements?

ME: Keeping them safe until the vampires return. We think that you are who we've been waiting for, but you must be worn out after that fight. I will have someone show you to a room. Then Drell will let you see the elements after you rest.

They get up and Drell takes them to a door on the side of the stairs. The door opens from the side and they walk in. The room has three beds and their gear inside. They go inside and sit down on the beds just looking at each other.

Jamal: You were right, wiped out. Over power, they still don't have in their possession.

Dom: Now I have reasons to kill every single one of them.

They get some rest and get up a few hours later; they walk out the room, and there the keepers stand waiting.

Drell: I hope you had some rest.

Dom: Yes and it was much needed, we thank you.

Drell: Good, follow me.

They rise to the surface in front of the rock, Drell walks up to the side of the rock.

Drell: This rock contains the elements, the elements where the powers of the most feared fighters in all of the vampire kingdom. They were called the seven; they were later known as the masters. We are here to see if you have the blood of any of them, if so you are vampires.

Drell pulls a weird key from his chest and touches the rock with it. A hand-sized scanner pad pops out.

Drell: Dominique, put your hand right here.

Dominique walks up and puts his hand on the pad which pricks him, taking some blood from his hand. The pad shuts and a door rises open in front of them. Drell walks in and the team follows him. Tan-ja and Nor-rock stand guard. They walk down some long stairs underground. Straight ahead, they see seven containers filled with glowing liquid. Drell walks up to an old-looking computer off to the side.

Jamal: How can we tell which ones are ours?

Drell: You will stand over there together in a small circle in the middle of the containers; I will start the process from here.

Dominique, Jade, and Jamal walk and stand in the middle of the elements, scanners come out the walls and scan them from head to toe. Clamps come out the ground around them and grab their wrist, waist, and legs so they don't move. A container moves behind each of them, Thunder behind Jamal, Fire behind Jade, and Electricity behind Dominique. A needle comes out of each of the containers and injects them through the spine. They all scream as the power is pumped into their bodies, shortly making them pass out from the pain. As everything turns black, they suddenly start to see themselves standing in the middle of a large clear patch in the forest on a sunny day. In front of them appears a large castle with long stairs that led up to two big doors in a kingdom of large homes surrounding them. Then vampires of all ages start to appear all around them walking toward the castle, a horn sound comes from the castle, and the doors open. Seven vampires walk out dressed in all black robes, each with their element on the chest, all with different blood stained weapons in their hands. Water is a male with nunchucks with blades on the ends, Wind is a female with a circular blade on a long chain, Electricity is a female with two blades that went along her arms and curved over the fist. The blade handles came out from the side and on the ends. Lightning is a female with a long jagged sword with the handle in the middle of the sword, Thunder is a male with a hammer on one end of a long pole and an axe on the other end of the pole, Fire is a male with two short thick poles with large spikes surrounding one of the ends of each pole, and Raw power is a male with a thick long sword with a blade the length of his body. As they line up on the middle of the stairs, an old man walks out behind them, dressed in a white robe with long white hair, and the people cheer. The team moves in toward the seven to get a better look at them, passing through the crowd of people as if they were ghosts. They walk up the stairs and see that behind the old man there are four men standing there in green robes. The old man puts up his hands, and the crowd calms down.

OM: The seven have yet again done what they were trained to do, defend against the constant attacks for our power. We show our thanks with this feast that our scientists tested and confirmed safe to eat. So this is a celebration not just for the seven but for all the warriors and every person on Mars. For this day is neither of war nor bloodshed, because this is a day of peace.

The seven and the green robes go down the stairs to eat and relax from the worries of war. They talk, dance, and just enjoy being alive. Then all of a sudden, the sky starts to turn gray, making the sun disappear. The team looks around and sees houses destroyed and bodies of vampires all over the ground with a heavy cloud of dust in the air, some badly injured from fighting and others sick with their flesh falling off trying to get away as wolves and sin-tars walk around shooting. An explosion comes from the castle; the team goes to check it out. They run up the stairs to see the castle doors ripped off the hinges, they proceed inside and see a young version of the high council running around breaking things in the castle. Seconds after, a wolf walks up to the council. He tells the HC something that sends him running outside while the rest of the council follow with the team running behind them. They run up to a well with dead wolves and sin-tars around it; a wolf stands there as the council run up.

The wolf: The seven killed all my men then went down the well.

HC: Find them now! I want their powers.

    Then he walks back to the castle with the rest of the council. Everything goes black, and they end up standing in the forest; they see the seven vampires running past as they avoid wolves and sin-tars running after them shooting. Lightning puts her hands out in front of her and strikes a group of enemies with a lightning bolt as they run through a clear part of the forest sending bodies flying into other enemy's shooting at them. The wolves that did not get hit keep shooting and running after the seven. Thunder turns and claps; a wave comes out from his hands that make enemies go flying into trees and rocks. As the seven run through the forest, they see a small group of enemies blocking their path running toward them. Electricity runs ahead of the rest of the team and at the enemies like a flash. In seconds, she ends up next to a wolf cutting off the wolf's head, and then she runs up to two other wolves hitting one in the stomach and slicing the other across the chest. The rest of the seven run off to the sides. Raw power runs up and swings his sword taking out a group of enemies cutting all of them in half with one strike. Water throws her blade and the chain wraps around the legs of a sin-tar making the sin-tar fall on top of a wolf running by. Fire ducks as a wolf swings at him, and then he stands up and swings a pole at the wolf. The spikes stabs the wolf in the chest, making the wolf slam to the ground.

Wind jumps and kicks a sin-tar in the chest then he lands and swings a nunchuck at the sin-tar, a gust of wind sends the sin-tar and everyone around him flying back. The seven regroup when they see they are surrounded, as the wolves and sin-tars move in to capture them suddenly the ground just opens up under the seven, They fall into the ground before it reforms, The wolves try to follow but can't. seconds later, they see the seven sit around with some Martians at the same table they were at. Raw power stands up to talk.

Raw: We can't let them have this world's powers too , we must hide it from them and who ever might steal it for war, we have to make them think we lost it.

Shortly after they wake up from the vision, the clamps come off and they go outside.

Drell: How are you feeling ?

Dom: I feel a tingling all over.

Dominique looks at his hand and sees the electricity flowing between his fingers.

Jade: I can since your body heat in the air.

Jamal: I can feel movement (as he swings a few times at the air).

Jade looks at Dominique noticing that the scar on his face was completely healed.

Jade: Dom your face!

Dominique takes a look at himself in a puddle of water. Jamal walks up to a tree and gets into a stance. He pulls his arms back and brings them together and claps. A wave comes from his hands, it hits the tree and other trees around it fall. Shortly after the team gets ready to head back out. They hear something coming up from their side, they look, and see its shadow. He's gotten bigger, now standing up to their calves with a longer tail. Later that night, they stand at the rock with the Mars Emperor, the keepers and Navell Saying their goodbyes.

ME: We hope to see you again.

Dominique walks up to Drell and shakes his hand.

Drell: Now that you know, what will you do?

Dom: What I have to do, what I was created to do, which is to protect my family.

The team say goodbye and follow Shadow to the west. They walk for miles until they start to hear some buzzing coming form a distance. They look up only to see a swarm of big flying bugs with large stingers fly toward them. Dominique and Jade pull their handguns and start shooting at the bugs, Jamal steps up with the cannon as the bugs get right above them and fires, the gun shoots out grenades. The grenades go off in the swarm hitting every bug, which fall to the ground. The team keeps moving toward the west. They walk for a few miles until Shadow leads them to a large fortress with two big doors. They hide behind some bushes to go over the plan. Dominique pets Shadow and he runs off.

Dom: Jade you take the south, Jamal you take the north, and I will come in from the roof.

They break off to find access points. Dominique gets to the roof and cuts a hole to get inside, then calls to check on the other's.

Dom: How we doing?

Jamal: I'm in.

Jade: Me too.

Dom: you know what to do. Set the bombs and get out.

Jade and Jamal: Yes sir.

They walk around the fortress setting the bombs all over the place. Dominique hangs on a walkway above another crossing walkway, he sees two beasts walking beneath both walkways. Dominique jumps down behind them without making a sound and then swings his sword killing them where they stand and sets another bomb. Jade walks into a room and puts a bomb under a table, hearing some voices as she leaves the room so she goes back into the room and hides under the table, something with black legs with claw-like feet and a fat black tail and a smaller person just like it walks in after.

SP: We can't get into their kingdom.

BP: Call a retreat and tell our brothers in the west we need day flyers.

SP: Yes sir.

Then they leave the room. Jade leaves the room shortly after and meets up with the boys. She shows them a video she shot when she was in the room under the table. They hide and wait for the rest of the beasts to come home. The beasts run from the east and go into the fortress. The door shuts, Dominique grabs a controller off his belt and sets the bombs. The bombs go off and make a big explosion that lights up the night sky. Some beast come running from the burning fortress, Jade walks up, puts up her hand and makes the fire hotter on the beast as she puts the flames out in the forest around the fortress. In seconds, the fortress turns to ashes. Still having time left before the sun comes up they trained their powers as they get ready to head back to the kingdom of Mars, they talk about what's on the video.

Jade: Should we tell them about these day flyers?

Jamal: And that theirs people west.

Dom: I'm not concerned with what happens to their people anymore; but let's just hope they didn't make that call before we took them out.

The team heads back to the kingdom, they walk in, and see the head of the council surrounded by amazons with one sitting on his lap drinking wine. The women leave the room when they see the team. The team sits down with the HC to debrief him on their mission. Some women bring in food for them as they talk.

HC: So how was the young one?

Dom:	she was a natural, like she was bred to do this.

HC:	That's good, so how was the mission?

Dom:	The shadow beast's nest has been wiped out.

HC:	Great, we will have a feast for this occasion this sunrise, now if that is all you can leave now.

The HC leaves the room stumbling, and the team sit's and eat. As they come to the end of the moon cycle, the team walks up some stairs. At the top they walk up to a table and see hundreds of people of the Mars kingdom standing around. The people cheer when they see them; the team half smile and wave and then sit down. The council sits to the side of them, the HC looks and waves at them as they wave back. Jade turns to Dominique.

Jade:	Maybe they have changed.

Dom:	We will see soon. I still think they want the elements, only if they knew it is right under their noses. I hope I'm wrong. Because if I'm not. there will be bloodshed.

They all go out after they eat to look at the moon go down and the sun come up. Dominique sits plotting their next move because he now knows the story.

CHAPTER 5

THE RIGHT ACTIONS

The next week, the team walks through the kingdom of Mars. As Jade shops, Dominique and Jamal talk.

Jamal: Since we've gained our powers, I've learned the true meaning of family, love, happiness. Through his eyes I can not only see it, I can fill it as well. To see how it was ripped away from him fills me with anger and sadness I've never felt before. They protected their people in the way we do, but all we ever get is glairs and side eyed. I'm even starting to recognize soldiers from my dreams. It's making me want to....

Dom: Me as well. Keep it calm, to their knowledge we know nothing, so let's keep it that way, (he puts his hand on Jamal's shoulder). We can't just go off, well not yet, we don't know what they have planned for us. But you will know when it's time because you will be able to run wild and I'll be right beside you when it's time to do what needs to be done.

Jamal looks at Dominique with a look of respect while shaking his head. Jade walks up and grabs them both by the arm, putting herself between them .

Jade: It's great to be alive (as she looks at the sun shining high in the sky filling almost like it's changing her).

They walk to a food cart as Dominique walks behind slowly grabbing his ear. Dominique could hear the high council from a tiny microphone he had placed in the leg of the HC chair when they were eating in the council meeting room. The council starts their meeting.

HC: Now that we are all here we can start. The shadow beast problem has been solved, and to make sure, we are sending scan bots to check the area for more.

CM s: So the mission was accomplished?

HC: Well, that's what they were created to do.

CM w: So what should we do with them now?

HC: We have started a project that's been long overdue. We have received four warriors that have been sent to become our new protectors, two wolves, a male and female; a sin-tar; and an amazon. They have all been put through similar training as Project Protect, making their fighting skill and thinking similar if not better to that of the clones. We will have the new team train with the clones. In that way, they will learn their ways and the Mars terrain before disposal. The new team should be ready for action by the next sun cycles. In other news, we have opened the case.

Dom: How did they do that?

HC: it seems that the case cannot stand high prolonged levels of heat, making the case soft enough to cut.

Dominion slaps his forehead shaking his head.

HC: Now we have all the enemy's battle plans and weapon designs.

Dominique walks up to Jade and Jamal.

Dom: I got something to do at the lab. I'll see you later.

Dominique runs to the back of the castle and gets on a bike. Dominique takes off toward the forest lab. He didn't want to concern the two of them yet. Jade was feeling good, and Jamal was already ready. He just wanted to be alone to think. As he rides along the edge of the forest, he starts to think about what he has heard and seen in the last few months, that's when he becomes angry, his body starts to glow with electricity. As he rides and as his anger grows, the electricity moves around faster around his body and then starts to fly off his body, hitting the ground around him. The dashboard of the bike starts to spark, sparks hits the ground, bounces back up, and hits the bikes gas tank. The bike explodes. Dominique gets tossed from the bike and into the forest like a rag doll hitting a group of bushes. Dominique gets up and feels his arm has been dislocated. He pops it back in without saying a word and walks the rest of the way. He makes it back to the lab and goes in. Shadow sits waiting for him and jumps on his lap when he lands on his chair.

Dom: Hey shadow.

Dominique grabs the case slamming it on a table, puts on some goggles, grabs a blowtorch, and then turns it on full blast. He waits for what seemed to be hours then turns the torch off. The case still looked the same to him, but he can feel the heat coming from it. Dominique pulls a blade from his belt, and then he pokes the side of the case. The blade goes through like cutting flesh. He gets inside the case and takes out the papers inside. He looks through the paper and sees battle plans and weapons that were made with materials that were not on Mars and a planet unknown to him called Valcanya. He drops the papers and goes to a room with a bed in it and lies down to think. Dominique shuts his eyes, and then he starts to sees the seven sitting on the ground around a fire with their legs crossed and eyes closed. He wakes up and then gets out of the bed, sits on the ground, crosses his legs closing his eyes. Dominique starts to see the electricity flowing in all the electronics in the room. He could see the one called Master Electricity standing before him and the powers her element gave her. He opens his eyes and stands up filling recharged. He runs out of the lab, grabs another bike from the forest lab garage, and heads back to the kingdom. Dominique gets back and walks up to Jade who is sitting on the back steps.

Dom: Where's Jamal?

Jade: Working out, he got restless.

Dom: Meeting at the forest lab. Be there in ten minutes.

Dominique gets back on his bike and heads back to the forest lab. Jade and Jamal meet him at the forest lab; they sit around looking at the papers.

Dom: They are bringing on a new team. They want them to take us out.

Jamal: So should we take them now?

Dom: Not yet, this new team makes no real difference, they're just an inconvenience. We keep on with the training of our powers. Because if we want this planet back, we must be prepared.

Jade and Jamal returned to the kingdom, while Dominique stayed behind to train.

CHAPTER 6

GETTING IN GEAR

Dominique returns to the castle the next day. As he walks into the castle, he looks around and imagines what used to be. He walks to his room and locks the door; he lies down on his bed and shuts his eyes. He starts to see as if he was flying over the planet like a bird on a sunny day; not the planet that he sees every day, but one that is covered by forest as far as he could see. He starts in the east and sees the vampire's kingdom where the kingdom of Mars sits now. Moving west, he looks to the south and sees something large around reflecting the sun's light. Miles away from the northeast, he sees a small clay mountain and next to it a few miles north, he sees a very large stone mouton miles out on each side with a kingdom sitting on a cliff. Dominique wakes up sweating. Looking around, he lies back down for a few minutes before getting up and going to the clubhouse. In the clubhouse, Dominique sits at the computer looking at a map of Mars but sees nothing he had seen in his dream. He stops and starts training to think more on the matter,

Dom: The wolves must have found a nice safe place and settled because they were too afraid to explore, the forest can be a dangerous place for a person of minimum training. Those kingdoms must still be there.

A few hours later, Jade comes down to the clubhouse from her room.

Jade: Hey.

Dom: What's up?

All of a sudden, some alarms go off. Dominique runs to the computer and pulls up the video outside. Looking at the sky, it shows a large dark cloud coming from the west toward the kingdom. Dominique and Jade gear up and then make their way outside and see these white hairless bird-like creatures with large wings and talons, skinny bodies, long necks, and tails with what looked like a nail hooked on its tip. The heads were like birds with razor-sharp beaks attacking the people in the kingdom. Dominique receives a call from Jamal.

Jamal: We have a problem!

He hears shots go off in the background.

Dom: We are on the way! Hang on.

A wolf runs toward them.

Wolf: Help me! Help me!

A flyer swings on speaker swings its tail at the wolf. The hook stabs the wolf in the rib cage, snatching the wolf from the side, and taking the wolf away. Dominique looks at Jade.

Dom: These must be the day flyers, don't let them near you.

They move fast toward Jamal's location. They run by a woman that gets snatched up seconds later. As they run by people avoiding day flyers, a group of day flyers spots them running and goes after them. They see the day flyers so Dominique jumps up on a long table, and runs on top of it alongside Jade who is on the ground. Dominique pulls a crossbow with a fat-tipped arrow on it and then shoots it at the day flyers. Jade then pulls her sidearm and shoots the end of the arrow, making it explode. The explosion hits the day flyers and some of them hit the ground dead. Dominique and Jade arrive at Jamal's location. Jamal sees them running up as he shoots at flyers coming at him. the team gets back to back.

Jamal: Glad you could make it.

They get surrounded by flyers, one flies by Jamal. He hits it, making it fall to the ground and then he shoots it dead. Dominique shoots at flyer and the arrow goes though its neck, it falls out of the sky hitting a flyer beneath it and take's them both to the ground, breaking its wing when they hit the ground with the dead flyer lying on top of it. Almost as soon as the day flyers came, they left. Dominique walks up to the flyer that broke its wing unable to fly away from being pinned down and was swinging its tail at him. He shoots it in the head with an arrow. Blood and bodies fill the ground of the kingdom. Now the team stands in front of the high council dirty with day flyer blood on their clothes.

HC: We have a new threat, so I will be making four new additions to your team. You will be able to meet them and train with them by the next sun cycle. That will be all, leave.

Later the team sits in the club-house.

Dom: I want you to use your powers every time you're away from the kingdom until we figure out how to control them. I want you to train your bodies and minds as well. The powers need someone strong in might and will to contain it, and that's what we need to be.

The HC and the HS sit in the HC office talking having drinks.

HC: Any word on their arrival?

HS: Still on course, same estimated time, what bothers you my old friend.

HC: I'm just getting this feeling we must dispose of them, mostly the oldest boy.

HS: If you want it done sooner, maybe we should have the clones take a walk west?

HC: Now that could be a good idea, those barbarians would never think we sent them and retaliate, ether they will take the clones out or the clones will be doing some more cleaning up around here. That's settled, it shall be done.

Back in the clubhouse Jamal works on guns in the gun room, while Dominique and Jade sit and talk.

Jade: I just find it interestingly idiotic how they expect us to train our own executioner's.

Dom: for sure they want us gone and the elements for themselves, so I think we should give it to them by taking them out before they have a chance to make their move. And know this, it not going to be over once their gone. We are going to need an army.

For the next couple of nights, they stand guard to see if any beast comes out but nothing happens so they decide to go into the forest to train, Dominique also showed them how to charge their elements. He called it the connection. As they stand around in a circle, Dominique tells them how it works.

Dom: Since our elements are from Mars, we have a connection with the planet, By doing this, you will recharge your powers and it also shows you how to use your power by seeing what the element masters could do with them. Now I want you to do as I do and do what I say. (He sits, they follow.) Close your eyes and clear your mind, just think of your element, what it is, what it can do, and its place in nature. The rest will come.

As they sit, they start to feel the chills come over their bodies once again. Jade all of a sudden could see the heat in everything around her. Jamal could see sound waves covering everything around him. And Dominique could see the electricity flowing through everything around him. They could see through the eyes of the masters of their elements. They started to see some battles they had against the wolves. The fighting style they used to defeat them, and how they used the elements to devastate the attacking force, the team studies the visions as if it was a training video. They open their eyes and stand feeling refreshed and refueled.

Jamal: Yeah! I like this (throwing a couple of punches in the air).

Jade: It's like I've been asleep for days (as she keeps stretching).

Dom: That's just one more thing we have over them (as he stands there with his arms crossed). Let's get back, it's getting late.

They park their bikes in front of the castle and proceed inside for their meal. As they sit at the table, a woman server comes out to bring in their food.

Jade: Will our father be joining us tonight?

Server: His words were to tell you that he had to finish preparing the paper work for the new team (then she walks out).

The next day, the team sits spread out along the west wall of the kingdom inside large gun towers. As the sun sits high in the sky they stay alert and in contact with each other through headsets.

Jamal: It's very hot (as he wipes his forehead).

Jade: I know. Isn't it great (as she stares at the sun)?

Dominique chills back with his feet up shaping a blade. He checks the blade and then puts it away. Jamal looks up to the sky.

Jamal: Something's coming from the south-west (as he looks around).

All of a sudden, the scanner goes crazy and a voice comes out of the scanner.

Scanner: Enemy's hundred yards in closing, fifty yards in closing.

The scanner counts down to the approach of the day flyers. As the day flyer gets closer, the team gets their guns in position.

Dom: Fire!

The team unloads. Not one of them miss the waves of day flyers trying to get past the wall of bullets. It lasts for only minutes but feels like hours. When it ends, everything becomes quiet and all they can hear is the screams of wounded day flyers on the ground around the gates of the west wall.

The team comes down from the guns. As Dominique jumps down pulling a sword cutting off the head of a day flyer before he lands. The head goes rolling passed Jade and Jamal as they kill other wounded day flyers. Minutes later they walk around with blood dripping from their weapons making sure all the day flyers are dead before walking away from the massacre.

CHAPTER 7

ENEMY OF MY ENEMY'S

On a hot windy day, the team sits around in a meeting room at the Mars kingdom's lab waiting for the head scientist. The HS walks into the room.

HS: greeting. As you already know, there are four new team members that you will be training and protecting with now, so let's go meet them.

They get up walk to the gear and weapons area to meet the new team. When they get there, the new team stands around talking. When they see the team, they slowly line up in front of them.

Dom: I am Dominique leader of the protectors. These are your team my associates and your team leaders, Jamal and Jade, you will follow our orders. They are placed to help you protect. Now your names.

Wolf man: I am Strike.

A tall athletic built older man

Wolf women: Vee.

A shot athletic young woman

Amazon: Karan.

A tall athletic woman.

Sin-tar: I am Mustang.

A young slim nervous looking man.

Dom: Now that we are acquainted, let's move.

All of them stand in front of an opening at the edge of the forest. Dominique and his team stand facing the new team.

Dom: This is the forest. Anything that lives here will attack you, so you must proceed with extreme caution. Being a new protector, you are only allowed to travel thirty miles away from the kingdom on and off duties which will consist of protecting the kingdom of Mars with your lives, combing the edge of the forest, and any maintenance that may be requested. Now, this is a game we like to play. I put four flags within a hundred yard radius; all you have to do is retrieve them and bring them back. Look out for what's in there as well as one of us, I mostly would like to assess your skill level. Now go.

The new team takes off into the forest. Dominique turns to Jade and Jamal.

Dom: Remember this is just practice. Go.

Jade and Jamal run into the forest jumping in the trees, Dominique fixes his boot then walks into the forest. The new team runs in formation through the forest and then quickly stops together.

Strike: Split up.

They all take off running in different direction. Karan walks through the forest looking for a flag, Jade sites her from the trees unnoticed Jade jumps down without making a sound but accidentally steps on a dry leaf, Karan hears the noise and quickly turns around. Jade hide behind a big rock before she is seen. Karan looks around finding nothing so she continues looking for the flag. Jade runs up behind her and throws a punch. Karan blocks it, but the blow makes her fall on her side. As Karan gets up, she tries to trip Jade. Jade jumps up and kicks her on the face, Karan falls back and rolls to her feet then she runs at Jade. Karan jumps and kicks at her. Jade blocks sliding back, as she stops sliding, Karan lands. Jade looks at Karan dusting herself off and then moves back into the forest. Jamal runs along the tree tops looking for someone to fight. Jamal spots Strike running through the forest on a path. Jamal runs alongside him. Jamal jumps from the trees and then lands on Strike's back. They hit the ground rolling to their feet. Strike runs at Jamal, Jamal jumps over Strike and lands behind him. Strike turns around to a kick to the face, Strike stumbles to the side and then Jamal kicks him on the chest. Strike slams into a tree and then sides down it. Strike gets up, keeping his eyes on Jamal, Jamal runs up to Strike throwing a punch at Strike. Strike ducks, Jamal hits a tree. Strike still ducking, gives Jamal a shot to the ribs. Jamal stumbles back and just looks at Strike and then Jamal takes off into the forest. Strike looks around for a second and then proceeds to look for a flag. Dominique sees Mustang walking and looking around, Dominique rushes Mustang from the side, making him fall and slide a few feet from where Dominique pushed him. Mustang stands up and throws a punch. Dominique blocks and knees mustang on the side, Mustang leans over in pain. Dominique hits him on the face, Mustang falls to the ground. Dominique kicks him, making him slide back, Mustang slowly gets up and then they run at each other. They lock up. Dominique kicks Mustang to brake free but it doesn't work. Mustang kicks Dominique on the chest. Dominique stumbles back, Dominique just looks at Mustang and then walks away. Mustang just stands there looking around. Dominique, Jade, and Jamal meet up in the trees to find the last new team member, Vee. They hear a loud screech come not far away from the west, so they go check it out. When they arrive, they see Vee fighting off a group of small gray big head monkeys with long strong tails about the length of two of them and a deadly poisonous bite that could kill a full-grown shadow beast within seconds. Dominique, Jade, and Jamal step in to help her. Now standing back to back, they fight off the monkeys. A monkey jumps at Jade and she kicks it out of the sky. All the other monkeys keep attacking. Monkeys go flying from kicks and punches from the team and Vee, the rest of the new team shortly arrive to help. It lasts for minutes until the monkeys that weren't killed run off.

Dominique keeps the training going and the new team backs off into the forest. At the end of the training, they all have flags sitting around ready to pass out from exhaustion.

Dom: So it looks like you all have what it take to protect yourself and the people around you (he stands looking at the new team). Good job, tomorrow we patrol.

Months pass and the new team still hangs in there after numerous attacks from the creatures that live in the forest. As they look out in their new treehouse base setting just above the trees line, a large room with windows for walls filled with computers, gear and weapons racks sitting on top of a tall fat pillar at the edge of the forest northeast. As they stand around, the system detects an incoming ship that quickly lands on the north sands. Dominique and his team come down from the base and take some bikes to meet the ship. The new team goes to the roof, grabs some jet packs and follows them. They get to the ship as the doors lower and out came a woman with the head of a triceratops with a short fat tail. Then two twin male raptors with long thin tails followed behind her, one with brown spots all over his body. Behind them a buff man with the head of a T-rex and a long thick tail and s tall man with the head of Kentrosaurus and a long tail with spikes at the end. They come out of the ship and stand in a formation Dominique and the triceratops start to walk up to each other stopping a few feet away from each other.

Dom: Greetings, my name is Dominique, head protector for the kingdom of Mars.

Triceratops: My name is Tri-sarh. I am the leader of team T-5 from Volcananya. We are looking for some of our property. It was stolen from us. We last tracked the ship to this solder system. We were hoping you can be of assistance.

Dom: You're more than welcome to check the desert and forest with the exception of the kingdom. We have very delicate people and having unknown guests would make them think we are not doing our job.

Tri-sarh: Thanks (she walks back to her team).

Kentrosaurus: So what did he say?

Tri-sarh: Nothing important. I think they are hiding something, let's look around. Keep your eyes open.

Spotted Raptor: Hay, aren't they vampires?

Tri-sarh: Could be.

Raptor: I thought they were extinct?

Tri-sarh: There's either more or we are looking at the last ones.

Dominique walks up to his team.

Strike: So what do they want?

Dom: Nothing of concern they just want to survey the area, just keep your eye on them and keep us posted.

Later Dominique, Jade, and Jamal sit around in the forest lab.

Dom: They're looking for the cases the wolves stole.

Jamal: So what to do?

Dom: I think we can use this.

Minutes later Dominique sits in the HC's office to talk about the recent visitors.

HC: Report.

Dom: We have a situation, but the new team members are doing great.

HC: What is it?

Dominique gives the HC a folder with pictures of the visitors in it. HC looks through the folder.

Dom: They're looking for the case we found in the ship. They say it was stolen from them, and they last tracked in this solar system

HC: So we are dealing with reptons.

Dom: What's a repton?

HC: They are very powerful warlords with extreme strength. Don't take these guys lightly or believe a word they say. This case is a big matter and could start a war.

Dom: What do you want me to do about this?

HC: Make sure they don't find anything, and if they get too nosy, take them out.

Dom: Yes sir (then he stands up). Will that be all?

HC: No, it's not. I have some information on the race that has all to do with the separation of you and your people; rumor has it, they are still living on Mars at the west end of the forest.

Dominique starts to have an unsure feeling as the HC tells him more information, after which Dominique goes to the clubhouse and tells Jade and Jamal about the information he had received.

Jamal: we should go check it out?

Dom: I want to, but I don't know, it could be a trap. I told him I'll take a look anyway.

Dominique gets a call on his radio.

Mustang: Mustang to Dominique.

Dom: What is it?

Mustang: We found a few camera at the edge of the forest watching the castle.

Dom: Don't tamper with them.

Mustang: Yes, sir. Mustang out.

Jamal: I get it, Help them find the answers they are looking for and maybe we will be able to have an army on our side.

Dominique knods in agreement, As night falls, Dominique, Jade, and Jamal gear up and head out to gather more information on the reptons. they stand at the edge of the forest looking out at the reptons' ship. Dominique sets up a small camera and then turns to Jade and Jamal.

Dom: I want scanners all over the place. I want to know when they move, where they're going, and how fast they do it. I also want you to hack their cameras I want to see what they see.

Jade and Jamal: Yes sir.

They take off to do what they were told to. Dominique sits and watches the repton ship. After a few minutes, the ship doors lower, and then they all come out of the ship. One of them lights a fire and they begin training. The twin raptors versus the T-rex and Tri-sarh versus the Kentrosaurus. They all standoff, the T-rex runs and jumps at the raptors. They move as the T-rex hits the ground, both of the raptors swing at the same time, the T-rex gets out of the way then strikes back, hitting the spotted one on the side of the head, making the raptor fall back. The raptor twists on his back using his tail to get to his feet, Tri-sarh runs toward the Kentrosaurus and then jumps, kneeing him on the chest. He stumbles back and swings his tail at her. She moves out of the way as his tail hits the ground, making small craters. Dominique walks out of the dark forest slowly clapping as he walks up to them. They stop to look at him.

Dom: Wow, you guys are impressive!

They walk up to him, stopping a few feet away.

Trisarh: Nice to see you again.

Dom: Likewise, the last time I didn't get to meet your team

Trisarh: This is Rip (pointing to the spotted raptor), this is Lash (pointing to the other raptor), this is Rex. (turning to the T-rex), and this is Reggie (pointing to the Kentrosauurus).

Dom: Now that I meet your team, you should meet mine.

Jade and Jamal jump from the trees and land behind him.

Dom: This is Jade and Jamal.

Tri-sarh: What can I help you?

Dom: It would be more like what we can help each other with. I was hoping maybe we could talk.

Tri-sarh: Before I hear what you have to say, I would like to see what of your skill.

Dom: Who did you have in mind?

Tri-sarh: Rex

Rex steps up.

Dom: Jamal, if you don't mind.

Jamal steps up. Rex and Jamal stand off as everyone stands around them. Rex moves in swing wildly. Jamal blocks and moves quickly to Rex's side. As they stand side by side looking at each other, Rex swing his tail and hits Jamal on the chest. Jamal stumbles back, Rex runs and then jumps at him. Jamal claps as Rex comes toward him, and the wave makes Rex fly backward hitting the ground and slide to his team's feet, Rex looks up at his team before they help him up.

Dom: So can we talk now?

Tri-sarh: Not quite yet. Your turn.

Dominique steps up and Tri-sarh as. She throws a few punches and kicks. Dominique blocks each one only stopping when Dominique grabs her foot, blocking a kick to the head with his eyes and hands glowing brightly. As she stands down, his hands and eyes stop glowing.

Tri-sarh: I was always told you're people were scrawny, and your fighting style is everything the elders of my planet say, and seeing thunder and electricity just proves it, you're vampires. What about her?

Dom: Oh, her. She is too hot to handle.

Tri-sarh: All right (with a smile), well let us talk, follow me.

They all walk onto the repton ship with the doors closing behind them and have a seat at a small tablet.

Dom: What can you tell me about vampires?

Tri-sarh: I don't know much, only what I've heard in stories. But there are people on my planet that have actually stood beside the seven in the war.

Dominique takes off his backpack placing it on the table.

Dom: This is what was in one of the cases, I can get the other one for you, but I'll need your help.

Tri-sarh: we will contact you in twenty-five hours, I'm sure my leader will want to meet with you.

Dominique, Jamal, and Jade head back to the Mars kingdom waiting for the call.

CHAPTER 8

PLAN IN MOTION

Aboard the repton ship, Tri-sarh stands in front of a monitor to contact an older man with a brontosaurus head.

Tri-sarh: Greetings my king.

Bronto: Greetings my dear! (His face lighting up after seeing her).

Try-sarh: Father, (looking around embarrassed).

Bronto: Apologies,(in a serious tone), Team T-5, what is your report?

Tri-sarh: We have one of the cases contents, the other one is being held by the wolves in an unknown location. And I think there is someone you are gonna want to meet.

She pulls up videos of Dominique, Jade, and Jamal fighting.

Trisarh: From what we know, they are the last three left, and he is their leader.

A picture of Dominique glowing takes over the monitor.

Trisarh: They work alongside the wolves and sin-tars for some reason.

Bron: Their fighting style is just like I remember, bring him and I'll see what he has to say.

Tri-sarh: Yes sir, Tri-sarh out.

Dominique, Jade, and Jamal stand by the edge of the forest talking.

Jamal: You think they are gonna let us go with them?

Dom: I'm going alone.

Jade: What! No.

Jamal: That's not a good idea, we know nothing about them.

Dom: I can feel they can help us find out more about what happened here, someone there knows more about our people, can't you tell? their fighting style is too similar.

Jamal pauses thinking about it before nodding his head in agreement.

Dom: Plus you have this cycle off. Stay out of site and keep an eye on the new team. The council will think I'm in the west.

Jade and Jamal: Yes sir!

Then Rip and Lash appear at the edge of the forest. Rip hangs from a branch, and Lash leans up against a tree waiting for Dominique. Dominique puts on a backpack, hugs Jade and shakes Jamal's hand then follows the raptors. Before he goes into the forest, he turns back to his team.

Dom: Get started on Project P-4. I want it up and running upon my return.

Jade and Jamal: Yes, sir.

Dominique takes off behind the raptors as they move through the forest with such poise. They get to the ship, where the rest of team T-5 wait outside for their arrival.

Trisarh: I guess today is your lucky day, you get to come with us.

Dom: Good.

They get on the ship and take their seats to get ready for takeoff with Reggie at the driver seat; the ship slowly rises and points upward.

Reggie: launching.

He pulls back a lever, the ship takes off like a bullet. Dominique looks out the window and sees everything getting smaller. He could almost see the whole forest. He looks west but his sight is blocked by clouds as they exit the atmosphere. In space he sees his home, a red-grayish planet getting smaller and smaller as the ship move farther away as well as a disconnection. Dominique sits back in his chair as they cut through space; he looks in amazement as the stars get brighter against the big dark void of outer space .

Reggie: Okay, going into hyperdrive (then he pushes a button on the dashboard).

The speed increases. Sticking to his seat Dominique shuts his eyes, relaxes, and starts to meditate filling the ship pass by an magnetic field. He learns through his visions that his element is stronger off Mars, but there is only a certain amount. Dominique starts to see some fights that Master Electricity had with a few reptons in the past, so he studies it. The ship stops before they reach a large bright blue and green planet. Reggie radios the base.

Reggie: Team T-5 to base.

Base: This is base. What's your 2-11?

Reggie: This is team T-5, we are requesting a landing. We have a visitor on board.

Base: You have room on spot 2-24.

Reggie: Coming in for the landing.

They move toward the planet entering the atmosphere, from the ship window Dominique sees a planet full of thick full trees, green grasses filleds and large volcanoes. They fly over hundreds of buildings and toward lot full of ships. The ship comes to a slow stop before slowly landing, they exit the ship proceeding to a security checkpoint before entering the kingdom walls, Dominique sees a large castle and hundreds of reptons standing along a path leading to the castle doors. Dominique looks around to see reptons staring at him as he walks down the path with Tri-sarh.

Tri-sarh: Welcome to Valcanya.

She places her hand on Dominique's shoulder only to receive a small electric shock, she quickly pulls her hand back. Dominique just looks at her with a slight grin. They get to a large set of stairs and go up the stairs until they get to two large doors. The doors open and they are welcomed by the repton's leader, an old muscular bonasorus man.

Bronto: Welcome (shaking Dominique's hand)!

Dom: It's a pleasure to be here.

Bronto: Come, let's make our way inside.

Inside they sit at a large table.

Bron: You must be hungry from your travel (he snaps his fingers).

Then some repton servants walk in the room carrying large plates of food.

Bron: I hear you have something to discuss with me, but before I hear you out, I want to know what type of skills you have in a fight.

The leader and Dominique get up and walk to a door.

Bron: Long ago, our father reptons fought alongside the vampires in some of the bloodiest battles in our history, after a while the vampires told us to stay away saving us from the attack that wiped then out.

The doors open and they walk outside on to a balcony looking down at the city of Volcanya. Reptons stand around a large ring located right below the balcony.

Bron: You will fight four of my guards and if you impress me, only then we will talk.

Dom: Sounds like fun (with a smirk).

Bronto: Tri-sreh will escort you to the ring.

Dominique jumps down from the balcony landing in a ring. He stands up slowly looking around at all the reptons cheering.

Bronto: Your first opponent. Fed stone.

A repton about Dominique's height steps into the ring. Fed swings at Dominique, Dominique blocks but gets hit with another punch on the face. Dominique stumbles, the reptons cheer. Fed runs at Dominique as he stumbles, Dominique quickly moves to the side and knees Fed on the stomach. As

Fed stumbles back, Dominique runs up and kicks him on the face, knocking him off his feet and throwing him out the ring hitting the ground out cold. The crowd erupts in cheers.

Bronto: Good, good. Let's see what else you have for us.

In comes a large T-rex shaking the ground as he walk into the ring. Dominique gets ready. Back on Mars, Jade and Jamal work in the forest lab. In front of them lying on a table is the body of the P-4 project. After renovating the abandoned lad, they came across a glass tube filled with a thick liquid and submerged in the liquid was a tall muscular man with long shaggy hair, still alive but non responsive. They get him and themselves washed up and put on surgery gear. After injecting him with anesthetics numbing the body, Jade grabs a knife and begins to cut down the middle of the chest, Jamal puts a clamp in the chest to pry it open. They start replacing some of the bones throughout his body as well as a few of his no longer functioning organs with artificial ones wired together, made from a few of the strongest metals available to the team, they place a chest plate inside his chest to protect his new organs, then begin to sew his chest back together. Back on Volcanya, Dominique and the T-rex stand there looking at each other, both bloody and beat up, they run toward each other, Dominique kicks a punch coming at him, and then he kicks the T-rex on the leg, making him kneel. Dominique knees the T-rex on the face, the T-rex falls on his back but gets up fast, the T-rex starts running toward Dominique, Dominique turns around running away toward a pillar at the edge of the ring with the T-rex right behind him, Dominique runs up the pillar and flips over the T-rex landing behind the T-rex stepping on his tail, and with the other foot Dominique roundhouse kicks the T-Rex on the side of the head, lifting the T-rex off its feet ripping off the piece of tail he was standing on, The T-rex spins in the air, hits the ground, and roll out of the ring. Everyone cheers in excitement.

Bronto: Very well done, using your environment, these next fighters I think will be more of a challenge for you.

Dom: If they are like the other two. we should just go inside right now, (on one knee out of breath).

    Rip and Lash step in the ring. Dominique stands up facing them with one on each side. Rip kicks at Dominique's head, Dominique blocks, Lash kicks him on the leg making Dominique falls to his knees, while Lash swings his tail at Dominique's face. Dominique grabs his tail and pulls him to the ground. Dominique elbows Rip on the ribs as he runs up, making him bend over. And then Dominique hits Rip on the face, making him fall to the ground, and Dominique punches Lash in the neck as he gets up, making him roll away. Dominique rolls to his feet. Meanwhile, back on Mars, Jade and Jamal finishes up the P-4 Project. With all body parts ready, they have to give the P-4 Project a jumpstart to get him up and running. They strap him into a chair and stick pads on his body that were connected to a machine. They turn it on and it sends small shock waves to start his heart. As the machine works on P-4, they wait. Back on Valcanya, Dominique stands there looking at Rip and Lash. As they look back, the leader yells from the balcony.

Bronto: That's enough; if you come inside, we can talk now.

Dominique goes inside and they enter a lounge overlooking the fields of Valcanya to talk.

Bronto: Now you are my kind of fighter, I have some good ones, but none like you, you fight like a true vampire. I have always been amazed of how effective the vampires skills have always been even at their smaller stature. Now, what can I help you with?

Dom: My team and I are the only vampires left, I have a feeling that the wolves created my team and I to locate the elements. We found them, and the answers I have been looking for about my people since my youth. I want revenge and to regain control of my true fathers planet. They are cowards, and they don't deserve to live on Mars or anywhere else for that matter. Now, would you be able to assist us?

Bronto: Maybe we can help each other.

Dom: Go on.

Bronto: I trained with the vampires years ago but there's many new soldiers that could use the first hand experience. You train my army and you will have them to complete your task.

Dom: How about I train three teams and they will train the rest of your army, for they would be all I need.

Bronto :   Very well.

They shake hands, closing the deal, while back on Mars, Jade and Jamal sit looking at the lifeless body strapped to the chair. P-4 starts to move a little, and a little more, then suddenly, he yells and breaks out from the strap, he stands up but passes out hitting the ground. They pick him up, lay him on a tablet to check his vital signs.

Jamal: He looks okay (as he reads the scanner).

Jade: We will just have to wait until he wakes up.

Back on Valcanya, Dominique is given a tour of their base, Dominique looks around to see a group of reptons training on the grounds and working on their ships, he's led to a room by Tri-sarh with stacks of files sitting on a table.

Trisarh: Here are some files of the teams you might want to train, see ya around (then she walks out).

Dominique has a seat as he starts reading the files. He walks out minutes later with some folders in his hand and then hands them to Tri-sarh, She gives them to a repton that walks away.

Dom: I guess this will do.

Dominique and Tri-sarh get in a cart to continue with the tour. While on Mars, Jade and Jamal sit around waiting for P-4 to wake up. He opens his eyes and slowly sits up, Jade walks up to him slowly. P-4 looks at them like he's ready to attack, Jamal pulls a handgun from his side and points it at P-4, Jade has Jamal lower his weapon.

Jade: Greetings! I am Jade, this is Jamal. We are vampires as are you, you are one of the last four left. We are on Mars, our home planet. Our leader is taking care of business but you will meet him in a day or two.

P-4: What happened, why can't I remember anything?

Jade: You were created here by a race called the wolves. They had a few problems getting you started and abandoned you. We found and restored you.

P-4 tries to stand up but falls, Jade helps him up and walks him to a chair to sit down.

P-4: Why can't I feel my body?

Jade: it might still be the anesthetics, but we had to make some adjustments to your body so you would be able to sustain movement.

P-4: Why did they create me?

Jade: Just like yourself, my brothers and I were all created by the wolves. They made us to find an great ancient powers called the elements, killing all the people from are bloodlines to get a hold of them, but the first to hold its power hid them, taking the location to their graves. We find them.

P-4: How long has it been since all this happened?

Jamal: Not really sure.

P-4 slams his fist on the steel table next to him, making a large fist print in the metal table.

P-4 just sits there rubbing hi head.

Jade: Maybe you should get some rest, we have a big day tomorrow. We must see how effective everything is working.

On Valcanya, Dominique walks into a room and sees the repton leader sitting at a table looking over the files. Dominique joins him.

Bronto: I only have two team folders. Do you only need two now?

Dom: No, Team T-5 will be the third team.

Bronto: That will be no good, they are my personal guards.

Dom: I'm sure you can find guards to fill in for the team for 2190 hours. I need your for this to make this work.

Bronto: Very well.

Dominique just smiles. The next day, Jade and Jamal arrive at the forest lab after checking in at the castle to find P-4 gone, they check the lab noticing some weapons missing also, Jade and Jamal gear up and head out into the forest to find P-4.

Jade: What is he thinking?

Jamal: Who knows. We have to find him.

Plan in Motion

As they make their way through the forest, Jade steps in a puddle of blood, looking at where the blood came from, they see a dead hog with its guts all over the ground. Near the castle in the forest, Vee makes her rounds, going farther than she usually goes wanting to explore, she hears a noise coming from behind her, Vee turns pointing her gun at the trees behind her seeing nothing so she keeps on with her rounds, unknowingly walking toward a tree that P-4 is hiding behind. She looks behind the tree, but P-4 is gone, Vee turns and keeps walking but as she turns P-4 knocks the gun out of her hands kicking her to the ground, Vee rolls back to her feet pulling a knife, P-4 pulls a larger knife. They run at each other and lock knives, as P-4 overpowers, Vee She kicks him on the leg making him drop his knife so she could roll to get away, P-4 tries to drop-kick her but misses, She swings at P-4 but he grabs her arm. Vee tries to swing with the other arm and P-4 grabs it too, She tries to get away but has no luck, P-4 head butts her on the face braking her nose making her pass out, P-4 starts to slowly stretch her out pulling on her arms; she screams from the top of her lungs, Jade and Jamal hear the screams from yards away and move toward it. Her arms rip from her body, her body falls to the ground, although armless she still try's to get away, P-4 walks up to Vee with her arms in his hands dropping one and with the other arm, he beats Vee almost to death, after beating her with in an inch of her life, he picks up his large knife, kneels next to Vee, and lifts her head by her hair.

V: Why . . . who are you?

P-4:   Why? Revenge, who am I, I take the name Riyin.

Then he starts to slowly cut V's head off, Riyin looks up when he hears something coming, Jade and Jamal run up but all they see is Vee's body, arms, and head laying on the ground.

Jamal: It had to be him. Let's keep moving.

Then they take off into the forest to keep looking for P-4. After hours of looking, they go back to the forest lab and see Riyin coming out of a room after taking a shower, he looks at them with a smile.

Riyin: Good, you're back.

Jade: You can't go out there like that, that's not smart.

Riyin: I had to get out of here into the fresh air.

On Valcaya, Dominique stands in front of team T-5 and two other repton teams standing at attention. Team J-7 and team H-10, as they get ready to head to Mars.

Dom: I am Dominique, and for the next 2190 hours my team and I back on Mars will be training you to become better fighters than you are now, The reason I picked you is because I've liked something about your skills, I just want to make that something better. I hope you're ready, Let's move!

Every team gets into a ship, Dominique rides with team T-5, the ships take off and head to Mars. As the ships move through space, Dominique meditates to see what he can learn to help him train the reptons. They get to Mars and land a few miles away in the north, they take carts from their ship and drive south to the forest lab, When they arrive, they see Jade, Jamal, and Riyin stand side by side waiting for him. He walks up to them and hugs Jade and Jamal.

Dom: Everything went well, I hope.

Jamal: Just fine, just more training.

Dominique walks up to Riyin and they shake hands.

Dom: Welcome my brother; I am Dominique. It's great to finally meet you.

Riyin: Likewise, I'm Riyin.

Dom: Now I want you all to meet some new sparring partners.

Dominique and his team walk up to the reptons. As they unload their carts into the lab, the reptons stand at attention when they see Dominique walk up.

Dom: Stand down, I just want you all to meet your team leaders. This is Jamal, Jade, and Riyin, my team. Now I want you all to set up camp. I will let you know our next activity after you rest.

CHAPTER 9

KEEPING UP WITH APERIENTS

The reptons set up camp along the edge of the forest to rest. Dominique, Jade, and Jamal go to the castle so Dominique could check in with the council. As they make their way to the castle, they encounter Mustang at the back steps of the castle.

Mustang: Greetings Dominique, I heard you were away on business.

Dom: Greetings Mustang; it's good to be back.

They shake hands then Dominique makes his way inside to meet the council. Dominique stands in front of the council to talk.

HC: Greeting boy, your back, how was your search?

Dom: It went very well, but I have to head back out. I just came back to get my team and some more supplies,

	I'm sure the new team can take care of thing from here.
HC:	Do what you must, and it has also come to my attention that V is missing
Dom:	We will try to find her.
HC:	Very well, you may leave now.

They leave and go back to the forest lab to rest, later the team walk through the reptons campsite.

Dom:	Attention!

The three teams get in formation, as the team lines up side by side behind Dominique.

Dom:	This is day one of your training; on Mars we have a problem, more of a pest. These pests are called shadow beasts. My team and I took out a beast nest on the east, but we think there's more. All of you will help us look west. One of my sergeants and me will be leaders of one of you're team's. Jade will be with team J-7, Jamal with team H-10, and I will be with team T-5.

Dominique turns to Riyin.

Dom:	I want you to be my one-man army and scout ahead. Go as far as you want.
Riyin:	Yes sir (then he takes off into the forest).

The teams gear up and move out taking different paths into the forest. After several hours, Jamal and his team come across a field of bones picked clean sitting on blood stained grass. Jamal calls Dominique on his headset.

Jamal: I think we are getting close to the nest, I am in sector 3-6-9.

Dom: Moving to your location.

The teams meet at Jamal's location, to take samples that give them a hit on the trackers, they move on braking back into groups to cover more ground, minutes later they emerge from the forest stairing down a very small crescent shaped mountain with a series of caves covering it. With the sun shining down on them, Dominique stands there just looking at the caves.

Dom: Rip, Lash, lighten up.

They start to take off some of their gear only carrying two weapons and a handgun. Dominique, Rip, and Lash start to climb the mountain reaching the middle going in. They walk around slowly and see that the caves are connected from top to bottom. Climbing up from inside They reach the top floor where there is walkways the rest of the way to the top. Looking down, they see a fortress on the other side of the mountain. They make their way down to the fortress. Dominique signals Lash to check out the roof, Lash comes back down seconds later.

Lash: There are a lot of them, but they are all asleep.

Dom: All right, let's set up cameras all over.

Rip and Lash: Yes sir.

They set up the cameras regrouping at the top of the mountain. Rip and Lash head back down as Dominique stands there staring into the west before heading back himself. As Dominique sits and rests, Jamal walks up to him being tossed a small handheld monitor.

Dom: The mountain might be the day flyers nest, can't tell really, but there's a beast nest behind it.

Jamal: Blowing it up might be cool to see, but making it a training exercise would be fun.

Dom: I can see the potential, let the teams know.

Jamal walks over to the teams.

Jamal: Listen up.

They stop what they are doing to hear Jamal talk.

Jamal: Now what we got here is called a swipe and clean, we will be taking out all enemies to take over their base, so try not to cause too much damage. We move night fall.

As the sun starts to set in the east, the forest becomes dark. Dominique switches on the night vision for the cameras, seconds later the fortress doors opens and the beast come pouring out the fortress into the caves.

Dom: It's time.

Jamal: Let's move!

Everyone run's into the caves as the beasts enter catching them off guard. Dominique walks in slowly behind them to check for damages, stepping over the dead beasts piling up on the ground of the caves. Jade and Jamal run the front line with their teams, Jamal on the south end and Jade on the north. Dominique's team takes the middle, working their way up. Jamal walks through with a shotgun, he shoots a beast in mid-air trying to jump at him. A group of beast runs up behind him, he turns around and claps at them, making a wave that sends them flying into the sharp walls that rip their bodies apart. Jade moves fast through a crowd of beast striking each one of them with a pressure point to stop their movement stopping when she gets to the end of the crowd, every beast falls to the ground as if they were dying from thirst as she walks away. The teams pour out of the caves and surround the fortress. They bust in but see it's just an empty room.

Jamal: This must be the resting area.

Dom: This will be our new base.

Jade slides down from the top of the mountain with two members of her team. They stop in front of Dominique and Jamal.

Jade: what's next?

Dom: Let's clear the surrounding area.

CHAPTER 10

AMONG KINGS

Later that night, Dominique, Jade, and Jamal walk around the caves with light's set up along the walls.

Dom: Nice, I like it.

Jamal: Right, we could hang curtains over the openings, place a few pillows along the wall, I could see it now, (jokingly)

Jade giggles.

Dom: After seeing this place, there was only one thing I could see us using it for.

Jade: Are we thinking the same thing?

Dom: If you're thinking we make an army of shadow dogs, we are. And this will be their rest area.

Jamal shakes his head in approval. They walk up to the teams sitting around awaiting orders.

Dom: I want all the trees cleared within a fifty-mile radius. I think I like it here.

As everyone scrambles all around the mountain and fortress, Dominique pulls out a whistle and blows it. no sound is made but he puts it away and joins his team. Jade stands in the middle of a thick part of the forest and puts her hands out to her sides heating up the trees around her, making the trees dry up, wither, and die, one of the reptons with her touches a tree for it to just fall over. Jamal stands at the edge of the forest with his back to the mountain, plants his feet firm on the ground, pulls his arms back as far as he could, then brings them together clapping his hands. A wave rips trees out of the ground, making trees and rocks hit other trees knocking them over. Dominique walks into the forest, gets on one knee placing his hands on the ground, releasing a large amount of electricity into the soil reaching the trees 50 miles around him. The trees blow up from the large surge, wood chips start to fall like snow. As Dominique stands up, Tri-sarh walks up to him.

Tri-sarh: Wow, such power.

Dom: It's easy letting it go, the hard part is keeping it in.

When they are finished removing trees, the ground around the caves become a vacant dirt lot, they have named the lot. Dominique sends some reptons to hunt for food and others to set up camp. Dominique, Jade, and Jamal sit together at the bottom of the caves meditating. After charging themselves they join the reptons to eat. They all sit around the long tables eating their fill. Dominique stands up with a cup in hand.

Dom: We struck a great blow to the beast, so enjoy your food and rest up (then he sits and turns to Jade). I'm gonna need some things from the forest lab.

Dominique sends Jade a list of supplies to her hand held computer. Jade and her team gear up and head out to the forest lab. As Dominique watches Jade and her team leave, he sees something from a distance running up toward him fast. Some of the reptons see what Dominique sees and point their guns at it.

Dom: Stand down!

Dominique could see it was Shadow from his glowing green eyes. Shadow runs up to Dominique. He has gotten bigger standing to Dominique's waist. Dominique goes to one knee to pet Shadow.

Dom: Good boy. you heard me, you still hungry? come on.

Dominique, Jamal, and Shadow sit around a fire. They talk as Shadow eats a pile of bones while Dominique and Jamal smoke, passing a pipe looking at the stars.

Jamal: I can't explain it, but I feel there are more of us out there, a whole other planet perhaps. full of vampires that could have gotten away from the war.

Dom: Let's hope they're on our side (then he blows out a big cloud of smoke), and not traitors.

Jamal: You hear from Riyin yet?

Dom: Not yet, but his life signs are doing well.

At the forest lab, Jade stands outside of the lab and pushes a button on her belt. The ground next to the lab opens up, and the reptons drive out in carts. One of the carts has two bikes strapped to the back; the other cart has guns and tools. Jade jumps on the side of a cart.

Jade: Move out!

They move out back to the lot. Dominique and Jamal walk around the west side of the lot with Shadow looking for signs of the day flyers.

Dom: I don't think they've ever been here. We will have to check somewhere else.

They see two carts approaching from the east. Jade and her team parks the carts and get out, the reptons get some rest; Jade joins her brothers. As she gets to the fire, Shadow runs up to her.

Jade: Shadow, you made it back (as she pets him).

Dominique, Jade, and Jamal sit around the fire; Jade puts her hand in and out of the fire unfazed by the heat.

Jade: So how is this shadow dog thing gonna work?

Dom: We can't be everywhere at once, so with shadow dog's we have someone we can trust looking out

	for us and also being guards when we start cloning more of our kind.
Jade:	You created Shadow, but is it possible with the equipment we have, and won't they be too young?
Dom:	I've thought of that too but after looking around the abandon lab, I found some of the equipment they used to create us. It's in bad shape, but it can be repaired. And after seeing how fast Shadow has grown in such a short time, I've taken some of his blood and created a growth serum that will speed up the aging process.

Shortly after Dominique checks the tools and weapons in the carts. Jamal gets up later and walks to the cart that Dominique is sitting on still checking the weapons, as Jamal walks up. Dominique tosses him a shotgun.

Dom:	Get two guys, we're heading south.
Jamal:	Okay (cocking the gun).

Dominique, Jamal, and the four reptons going with them get geared up and ready to head out under the light of the full moon. They walk in formation, covering the areas all around them with Dominique in the lead as Jamal brings up the rear. After hours of walking through thick forest, they get to a thin part of the forest. As they keep walking, the ground gets soft and wet. Dominique sees a bright glare coming from the bottom of a slope, they keep walking and see that they stand at the end of a large swamp that stretched to the east of them.

Dom: We have a swamp!

Dominique tracks how deep it is by tossing a tracker in the water. Dominique and Jamal take off most of their gear and put on some helmets for underwater use to find out what lives in the water. After checking the headsets in the helmets they jump in leaving the reptons up top. The top of the swamp was filled with seaweed which made it hard to see. Going farther down in the water, it becomes clear. As clear as being on land. They swim around for a few hours and then sit on a large mountain in the water to rest their arms and legs. They start to fill something coming up behind them. They hide by the mouth of a large cave. A group of people with gills on their necks, sharp teeth, finger and toenails with sharklike skin, and webbed feet swim overhead, as they lay low, a bunch of rock start to float behind them. Dominique turns around slowly. Shining a lights, he sees the rocks.

Dom: Rocks don't float.

Jamal: What? (as he turns).

They sit and look at the rocks. All of the sudden, the rocks open what looked like eyes and mouths.

Dom: Thows are not rocks.

Their eyes were small and red, and their teeth were really sharp and long. Dominique and Jamal just stand there stuck, and then they take off out of the large cave as fast as they can swim with the rocks following close behind them. The rocks nip at their heels as they swim for their lives. Dominique shoots some electricity at the rocks. Some of the small rocks fall, the bigger ones shake it off and keep coming. Jamal swims ahead of Dominique, and Jamal looks back at Dominique.

Jamal: Grab my foot.

Dominique grabs him, Jamal puts his hand behind him and with both hands snaps his fingers making waves that send them cutting through the water. Dominique looks at his foot and sees it in a rocks mouth, using his power Dominique shoots it off and they keep going. They slow down and stop miles away. They rest and then keep moving until they come across an underwater kingdom. They move in slowly trying not to be seen. They see that it is covered by what looks to be a big bubble, keeping the water out but letting people walk through it. As they sit and watch, some of the underwater people dressed in what seems to look like rock armor with rock weapons surround and take them in. Dominique and Jamal walk chained up, surrounded and escorted by guards through the kingdom to the castle. They see hundreds of underwater people of all different sizes and ages in a kingdom made out of rock and silver. They get to the castle and go in. They walk into a large room surrounded by a balcony. They are taken to the middle of the room. Above them sits a large stocky underwater man with a silver crown on his head. He sits kicking back on his thrown until he sees Dominique and Jamal. He gets up and walks to the edge.

A guard: My king, we found these two wondering around outside the kingdom.

King: Well done, unchain them.

The guards let them go before taking them to a lounge filled with couches and pillows where they have a seat. The king walks in, they shake hands, sit, and talk.

King: Welcome to my kingdom, I am King Razor, leader of the Sharkins,

Dom: Greetings! I am Dominique, and this is my brother Jamal.

Razor: What is it you are looking for?

Dom: Nothing, we were just exploring.

Razor: Tell me this. are you vampires?

Dom: From what I hear, yes we are. Why did you let us go?

Razor: I can tell you work for the wolves, but you live for yourself, plus they would have sent an army. My father used to tell me stories of the great and powerful vampires and a group of them that controlled elements of Mars, known as the seven, a race that was cheated out of a full life. My people have lived here for as long as I can remember alongside our serfus brothers, the Gators. The story is that we are the children of refugees from a planet destroyed by the wolves after my grandfather refused to fight alongside them because of the company they kept. We later found out after our scouts returned to tell us that they hooked up with some people we know as shadow warriors here on Mars. The king did not want anything to do with the war, finding out my people felt the same he granted us asylum, but his son, the prince, did not like that the vampires gained the power of Mars and wanted them gone. The prince later allied himself with the wolves and created a type of beast that lived with a disease. Those things out there called the shadow beast. The vampires found out too late of this union, only after they set their plan and set the beast free into the forest, forcing the vampires to use the beast as food when the beast started to eat everything in the forest. And that's how I heard it all happen. We thought there were no more vampires until now.

Jamal: we've heard of these shadow people. In the west, Right?

Razor: Yes, in the west, but these aren't the type of people that you would want to meet. During the war, the prince overthrew the king. They aren't like they were before. They have become more barbaric throughout the years, but we keep them and their beast at bay.

A Sharkin woman walks into the room.

S woman: King Iron Jaw would like to speak with you (then she leaves).

Razor gets up.

Razor: Come with me, I have someone I want you to meet.

They walk down a long hallway into a garage area containing large digging carts and tools. At the end of the room sits a large cave, At the mouth of the cave stand three rough scaly skinned men with webbed feet and hands, sharp teeth, finger and toenails, dressed in what looked like wood armor. A short athletic man with long dreads walk's up to Razor as they approach them shaking hands with one hand, placing the other on each other shoulders.

Razor: King, what might the problem be?

I jaw: Some of my people captured some reptons on the surface. What do you know about that?

Dom: My apologies, they're with me.

I jaw: And you are?

Dom: I am Dominique, leader of the new vampires.

I jaw: Cool, I'm King Iron Jaw, leader of the Gators.

They shake hands and Iron Jaw takes them to the reptons. They walk through the cave exiting out the other side on top of the water inside a very large castle made of wood and gold. They walk down a hallway to a cell were the reptons are being kept, looking in bad shape. Dominique calls for a pick-up. An hour later, Jade comes and picks up the reptons and Jamal. Dominique stays behind to talk more with the kings. They go back to the Sharkin castle talking and drinking wine. Later, Dominique is given a tour of the castle. They walk up to a large door entering.

Razor: This is my favorite room in the place.

They walk into a large dojo with rock weapons hanging all over the walls. Iron Jaw stumbles to the middle of the room.

I Jaw: Dominique, I've heard of the instinct a vampire has in a fight. I wanna see it.

Dom: Sure, (walking up to Iron Jaw).

Dominique and Iron jaw stand facing each other, Iron Jaw takes off his wood armor. It hits the ground sounding like rock hitting rock. Back at camp, Jade looks over the reptons as they work. As they rest, she overhears a group talking.

Repton: I don't know what this has to do with becoming a better fighter.

Jade: Almost everything. If you're in someone else's backyard, you have to be ready to adapted, figure out how to change the playing field or you're just playing their game, and it's no fun if you can't show them what you got.

Back at the swamp, Razor sits watching in amazement as Dominique and Iron Jaw trade blows. Iron jaw runs at Dominique and swings, Dominique ducks and hits Iron Jaw on the chest with an elbow, making him stumble back. Dominique runs at Iron Jaw. Iron Jaw kicks Dominique on the hip, Dominique loses the feeling on his leg jumping up and down to get it back. Iron Jaw comes again with a swing. Dominique blocks him, grabs his wrist, and pulls him close, giving him a knee to the ribs. Iron Jaw stumbles back, holding his ribs. They walk around keeping eyes on one another then run at each other again. They both swing and hit each other on the shoulders. They both fall to the ground busting in laughter. They lay there drunk for a few minutes before getting to their feet and shaking hands. Dominique walks up to one of the walls.

Dom: You mind?

Razor: Go ahead.

Dominique grabs a Bo staff instantly noticing its smooth texture and heavy weight. Dominique spins it behind his back over his head and then flips with that staff. It slips out of his hands and goes flying toward the kings. Dominique reaches for the staff. Using his power, he stops the staff in mid-air right above the kings heads and then pulls the staff back to his hands.

Razor: Wow, (clapping his hand slowly almost falling out of his seat) that was amazing. I heard my father talk about the element but to see one of them. Your Electricity, the only element that can control it.

Dom: What are your weapons made out of, and your armor isn't rock or wood is it?

Razor: It's a mineral. Well, let me show you.

Dominique and the kings go to the cave entrance, they get in a cart and drive down a long steep tunnel. As they go deeper, a bright light starts to shine from within the cave. Dominique starts to feel the same chill as they get closer along with a pulse from a beating heart. Upon exiting the tunnel Dominique sees a large glowing rock coming from the ground in the middle of the cave pulsating. Dominique could fill massif amounts of power coming from the rock with each pulse.

Razor: This is the heart of the planet, it is the power source powering our kingdoms. Long ago when our people came to this planet, the vampires helped us build our kingdoms and told us to protect the hart of power, and that's what we've been doing ever since.

Iron Jaw walks up to the rock and breaks off a piece, Dominique notices that the rock instantly grows back. Iron Jaw walks back over to them and hands Dominique the piece of rock. Dominique just looks at the rock as he holds it in his hands.

Iron Jaw: intoxicating, isn't it? In this form, its soft enough to mold. It is twenty times stronger than any metal in the galaxy, and each piece contains its own power source. Good stuff.

Dominique tries to hand it back.

Iron Jaw: Keep it; it as a gift.

Dom: Much appreciated.

Done talking, they stand in front of the gator's kingdom to say their goodbyes. Dominique stands next to a bike that Jade left for him. Dominique fixes his new weapon on his belt, a custom knife, an eight-inch dual-edge blade with a finger grip handle and a finger-sized hole at the end of the handle. Doom was carved into the blade. He put Doom on the blade because that's what he was going to bring to all of his enemies. The knife still with its Raw power appearance.

Dom: You're both great kings, I can't wait to fight beside you.

Razor: You will be as well, my brother.

Iron Jaw: I know it will be a blast.

Dom: Maybe we can do this again.

Iron Jaw: I will let you know when my ribs heal.

Dominique gets on his bike, rubbings his leg as he laughs. Under the bright moon, Dominique rides back to the lot. As Dominique rides, the Doom knife starts to glow brighter before transforming into a shiny black steel.

CHAPTER 11

LOOSE ENDS

Dominique makes his way back to the mountain to debrief and check the construction.

Dom: well done.

Walking around the fortress with Jade.

Jade: everything has been done to your specifications.

The fortress now has more rooms with sliding doors, a few labs, an underground meeting room, mess hall, and rest area. Around the lot, they also set up gun towers facing each direction. As Dominique walks around, he gets a call from Riyin.

Riyin: I'm coming back, I got something I know you'll want to see.

In a meeting room, Riyin pulls out a camera and hooks it to a monitor. They see Riyin walking in the dark forest with the camera's compass reading west. He sees a very large stone mountain that stretches across the forest from north to south. He walks up to the mountain, and then the camera goes off.

Seconds later, the video comes back on, with Riyin on top of the mountain looking down at the trees but his site is blocked by heavy fog, he walks north until he comes across a dark stone castle on a cliff. Riyin moves in closer and then zooms in with the camera. Then walking out from the darkness, he sees a bald tall muscular man with pitch-black skin, long thick tail and clawed feet. Riyin zooms in more, suddenly the man looks into the camera. Riyin starts to run back, and then the camera cuts off.

Dom: Okay, just like everyone's been telling me.

Jamal: So we move with the reptons

Dom: I don't want them to think it's an attack. We move when the sun comes up.

Dominique and his team use the time they have left with the reptons to train hard. By the end, Dominique and his team brake four reptons rib cages, three legs and gave two minor concussions. At the end of the training, the reptons skills are ten times better all around than upon their arrival. As the sun comes up, the reptons leave Mars and head back home. Jade and Jamal hang around the lot as Dominique takes Riyin to the cave of elements. Dominique and Riyin pull up to the cave, meeting the keeper's of the elements.

Riyin: Who are they?

Dom: Some of the best allies a warrior can have.

Dominique and Drell walk up to each other and shake hands. Later, Riyin and Dominique stand facing each other ready to fight. Riyin runs at Dominique and throws a few punches. Dominique blocks each one and then kicks Riyin, making him stumble back.

Dom: Come on Riyin, show me something!

Riyin jumps at Dominique, Dominique moves out the way. Riyin's fist hits the ground, making a large hole making Dominique smile, Riyin comes at Dominique and swings again. Dominique backs up to a tree and ducks, Riyin takes a chunk out of a tree. Dominique swings hitting Riyin on the ribs. Riyin just stands absorbing the hit and then swings with the other arm as Dominique stands up. Dominique blocks but is pushed back sliding several feet. Dominique shakes his arms filling the massive amount of power behind the punch.

Dom: Now that's what I'm talking about.

Arriving back at the lot, Riyin helps Jade work on some carts, and Dominique rewatches the video. Jamal walks into the meeting room.

Jamal: we ready to move?

Dom: Not yet, give me a few more hours, then we can roll.

Jamal: Good, That gives me time to finish what I've been working on.

Later Dominique stands outside with Jade and Riyin as they train their powers on the west end of the lot. Jamal comes out from the fortress with a small gray metallic rifle in his hands.

Dom: So what have we got here?

Jamal: I call this the jay-gun. This gun shoots three rounds every time you pull the trigger. On impact, the rounds scatter hitting other nearby targets. Let me show you.

Jamal shoots once at a tree hitting dead center, creating a large hole. Behind the tree sits a rock with chunks missing and imbedded in other trees around it. They all clap for Jamal as he takes a bow.

Jamal: I also made same rounds for our handguns as well. ready when you are.

Dom: Well, let's gear up and head out.

The team dressed in all black gear get on black steal bikes, each of them carrying a jay-gun and their weapons of choice. Jamal with two shotguns strapped to his back and four handguns in belt and leg holsters. Jade a retractable bo staff and a dagger on her hip with two handguns in leg holsters. Riyin with a short thick sword strapped to his lower back. Dominique with two swords on his back, one long, the other short and his Doom knife in a custom made leg holster. Jamal notices a small pouch tied around Dominique's waist.

Jamal: What's that?

Dom: O this. It's a peace offering incase they don't want to be friends.

Under a overcast sun on a cold wet day, they head west to the Stone Mountain. After riding for a few miles, they noticed north of them, they are passing by a small clay mountain right above the tree line, with what looks like large cannon's lined up sticking out from the side of it, but keep riding a few more miles until they reach the Stone Mountain. They hide their bikes and climb up to the castle, they get to the castle checking the area making their way to the doors. They open the doors to see a long hallway lit by torches. They walk down the hallway until they get to another door and open it to see a large ring surrounded by stone bleachers, directly ahead just above the seats hangs a balcony holding two thrones made of stone, no other doors seem to be present in the room. When they walk in, the doors close behind them. They look around to suddenly see the same man in Riyin's video, standing between the thrones.

Shadow man: You are trust passing in the kingdom of the Great king lord Pakeya,

Dom: Okay. We are looking for the ones they call shadow warriors.

Pakeya: Then you came to the right place. What is it you want?

Dom: We're from another planet and are seeking the aide of fierce warriors in a war we are fighting. We heard your people are the force behind the extinction of the vampires.

Pakeya: That is correct!. Those runaways got what was coming to them, stealing our birth rights. And the price for that, Their bones and flesh now make up the sands. Are you impressed. Or do you require a trial-run?

Dom: I've always wanted to see what a vampire killer can do. Let's.

Pakeya snaps his fingers, hundreds of shadow people come from out of the shadows in the seats all yelling and cheering. Then out of a shaded area in the ring walks up a tall man with steel-spiked armor on, carrying two long swords. Dominique steps up, the man quickly attacks jumping in the air, swinging his swords downward at Dominique making him roll to the man's side, pulling his short swords, as the man swings for his head. Dominique blocks then front-kicks the man on the chest. the man stumbles back swinging his tail. His tail knocks Dominique's short sword out of his hand and across the room. Dominique avoids numerous hits as he trying to reach his sword. The man swings from the side, Dominique jumps and rolls over a swing from the man's tail picking up his sword, landing on one knee. The man then swings both swords downward at Dominique. Dominique blocks the hit with his short sword, at the same time pulling and swinging his long sword, cutting the man in half at the waist. The man falls down sinking into the ground.

Pakeya: So I see you have some skill yourself.

Pakeya takes a seat on one of the thrones waving his hand, and then out of the stands, a woman jumps down into the ring. Jade steps up.

Jade: My turn.

The woman pulls out a whip with a large ball of spikes at the tip. Jade pulls her bo staff making it grow. The woman cracks the whip at Jade twice. Jade moves from side to side avoiding the cracks of the whip. The woman swings the whip at Jade wrapping the whip around Jade's staff. They both pull until Jade lets go and at the same time starts running at the woman. As Jade and the staff reach the woman, Jade grabs her staff and swings for the woman's head, hitting the woman on the face with her own spikes killing her. She falls and is gone too.

Pakeya: his has me thinking of something. You two have a fighting style I've seen before. So precise, inventive, and kind of delightfully brutal, to be honest. I know. You must be survivors. Turn them to dust!

Before Jade could make her way back to the rest of the team, people jump down from the stands. A very large monster of a man, wearing armor on only one of his arms carrying a large ball and chains, jumps from the stands and blocks Jade off from the other's. As Jade fights her way to the guys, she comes face-to-face with the monster-man. As he swings at her; she rolls under his legs, before making her way to the guys, she knocks a man out that was charging at Riyin, They pull their jay-guns and fire, knowing people back from the rounds. Jamal and Riyin open the doors, the team backs out slowly still shooting at the mob. Jamal claps at the people coming at them, sending them flying back into each other. Jade and Riyin close the doors as Dominique and Jamal keep shooting. Right before the door is shut all the way, Dominique rolls back inside jamming the door with his short sword. As the team try to get the doors open, they hear Dominique coming threw their headsets.

Dom: Get back to the lot now!

They all take off running to get outside. Dominique shoots at the shadow warriors, kicking and punching people running up to him. Dominique runs out of bullets in his jay-gun chucking it hitting someone in the head, then pulls out a handgun and the Doom knife. Dominique shoots a man running up to him and then chucks the knife at someone from far away, killing them. The monster man approaches as Dominique pulls the knife back to his hand. Dominique suddenly lets out a large amount of power from his whole body, sending the buff man flying into the seats. Dominique then takes off his helmet throwing it at someone. Dominique and Pakeya lock eyes, Dominique then takes off the pouch and throws it at Pakeya. Pakeya catches the pouch inspecting it. Dominique still fighting people around him, starts to move at a faster pace then everyone in the room, lines up a shot at Pakeya face and fires, sending a bullet flying toward him. Pakeya instinctively blocks the round with the pouch, not knowing that the pouch contains a very high level of explosives. The bullet hits the pouch, creating a huge explosion, everyone in the room are covered by flames. As the team makes it out of the castle, without warning the castle explodes. The explosion knocks them off their feet sliding toward the edge of the cliff. Jade stands up screaming.

Jade: Dom! Dominique! (falling to her knees crying).

They spend some time looking through the debris finding nothing, then climb down and making their way back the lot. Hours later, Dominique pulls himself from underneath the rubble, bloody and badly burned to the point of disfigurement, with a busted leg, and a severed arm up to the elbow. Dominique claims down taking some time do to his injuries, trying to ride going in and out of consciousness. As Dominique rides through the forest, a large spiked steel ball hits him on the chest, knocks him off the bike, sending him flying back hitting the ground hard. The bike keeps rolling until it hits a tree, exploding on impact, Dominique drags himself up against a rock. Loking down at his chest, he sees blood pouring out of a large deep gash exposing his rig-cage as electricity moves around inside his body. As Dominique lays there unable to move, the monster-man approaches him, covered in severe burns with smoke coming from his body, swinging the ball and chain around above his head. As the man goes to strike Dominique, a woman dressed in a white dress and steel boots with a long sword in her hand and a handgun on her waist jumps out from the forest kicking the man on the ribs, making him stumble to the side. The man runs at her swinging, she rolls under his arm cutting it off. The man yells as his arm, ball and chain hit the ground. The man swings his other arm at her, she ducks then rolls to the side as he runs past her. As the monster-man turns around, he is met by her cutting his head clean off. The head rolls to Dominique's feet, as the body drops sinking into the ground. The woman walks over to Dominique as he keeps falling in and out of consciousness. Dominique sees a young beautiful woman, She looked like an amazon but not like the ones back at the kingdom, because this woman has a pearl in the middle of her forehead. She checks out Dominique's wounds.

Woman: Hey, you all right?, well your still alive.

Dominique passes out. At the lot the, the team sits in the meeting room.

Riyin: What do we do now?

Jamal: Exactly what he would do.

Jade and Jamal make their way back to the kingdom. They stand in front of the council, Jade trying to fight back tears.

Jamal: I regret to inform you that Dominique. Was killed in the last mission.

HC: Are you sure of this?

Jamal: Yes, sir.

HC takes a good look at Jade.

HC: Then there will be a ceremony in his memory. That will be all.

Jade and Jamal leave. Jade goes to her room and Jamal goes home. The council stays to talk.

CM s: Now that their leader is gone, what should we do with them?

HC: Have you forgotten, we don't even have one element. Let them be, they will do all the dirty work. It might be okay for us to keep them around without their leader, and with the right guidons I feel they will become great weapons for us in the future.

CM wolf woman: we were told to only hold this planet.

HC: would you rather be the ones that held the planet, or. The ones whom prepared it?

The rest of the counsel nods the heads in agreement. As the moon falls and the sun rises, the people in the kingdom all stand outside around the castle steps.

HC: A great protector died the other day, doing what he was born to do. This day should not be a sad one, for he made this place a safer place to live for all of us. So we honor the man we know as Dominique.

Everyone in the kingdom go back to what they where doing, as if the HC just made an announcement. Jade and Jamal keep going on with the plan by finishing up with the shadow dogs. Following Dominique's notes, they make three pups and ship them to the lot to be trained by Shadow. After a few weeks the dogs become efficient hunters and guard dogs. The team sits in the lot meeting room to talk plans.

Jamal: Now what we have to do is more important than it was before. We are now moving on to creating an army.

The team prepares for cloning, Dominique's lays in a bed, in a room made of clay, covered from head to toe in bandages. Dominique opens his eyes no longer filling pain and hops out of the bed taking off some of his bandages, to see he has completely healed. He sits down on the bed rubbing the back of his neck, The woman from the forest walks into the room with a tray of food.

Woman: I see you're up. My name is Daisy, and this is the amazon kingdom.

Dom: My name is Dominique. How long have I been out?

Daisy: almost three cycles.

She sets a tray of food next to Dominique. Daisy leans over taking off the rest of his bandages. Dominique inhales her sent, it suddenly makes his heart start to beat fast.

Dom: How did you heal me?

Daisy: I did nothing, you're powers did that. I could feel it, that's how I found you.

Dom: That must be why I feel stronger. How do you know about my powers?

She takes a seat in a chair in front of him, as Dominique eats.

Daisy: My mother still tells us stories about the vampires and a strong and powerful group of seven that we owe our lives to. She has been waiting for you to wake up.

Dominique puts on clothes and they leave the room. Dominique steps outside to see that the room is one of many that have been carved into the clay mountain exiting on to long balconies that connect by staircases to the ground floor, all over the clay mountain, surrounding two large stone doors at the center of the kingdom, he sees hundreds of beautiful women dressed in white, walking and working around the kingdom, Dominique notices that only the women about Daisy's age and younger have the same pearls in their foreheads. As they walk down a path, the women stare at Dominique as he looks back. They get to two large doors on the clay mountain, the doors open, and they go in. Inside is a large room with windows on the ceiling and back wall, an older beautiful woman in a long white dress sits on a throne.

Daisy: Mother.

Woman:	Daughter, (then turns to Dominique), I'm glad you could join us this day. How are you feeling?
Dom:	Much better, thank you.
Woman:	I am Janell, queen of the amazons. I see you already met the princess. And this is our kingdom.
Dom:	You look like the amazons back at the kingdom of Mars.
Jan-ell:	We are one and the same, but the difference is that their daughters would be of wolf and sin-tar blood, and many like Daisy are from the bloodline of the vampires.
Dom:	I see.
Jan-ell:	The women you've seen are a result of amazons that chosen to be captured again during the war.

The queen gets up and walks to the windows behind her, they follow. Dominique looks out the window and sees a field of green grass and under the window a small lake.

Jan-ell:	We can't thank you enough for taking out the shadow warriors for us. They have been a pain in our sides since we came to this planet because of the war.
Dom:	It was my pleasure; it was just one thing I had to take care of before I take out the kingdom of Mars. So you're telling me you're not from this planet?

Jan-ell: Not all of us, the amazons close to Daisy's age are native to this planet, but the ones my age, we like many also bear witness of the wolves' conquest for power and the lives and homes lost as a result of the search. We owe our lives to the vampires. Years ago, my home world was conquered by the wolves and their allies. Some were able to escape finding Mars and the vampires, they gave us a home here along side them, here in this very kingdom, and after our first born became of age to be trained…

Daisy: We learned that the pearls on our heads could tell us what people's intentions are, and it shows us what a person's going to do seconds before they make a move.

After they talked to the queen, Dominique and Daisy walk around the amazon kingdom lake talking.

Dom: I have to get back to my team, it's been too long.

Daisy: So there's more like you?

Dom: Yes, three others.

Daisy: And do they possess an element as well?

Dom: Yes they do. Is there any chance we could have allies within the kingdom?

Daisy: I doubt it, the one's who departed, did so, do to a power struggle over leadership that started with ugly battle, ending enough life's, that a one on one match was the deciding factor placing my mother on the throne.

Dom: So no luck there.

Daisy just shakes her head looking at Dominique. Now Dominique stands at the front gates, ready to leave surrounded by women hugging and kissing him.

Daisy: Anything you need, you can come to us. We will be here.

They shake hands and Dominique heads east along the edge of the forest to the lot, feeling lighter he starts to run. As he runs, he picks up speed. It takes him an half hour to get back on foot, what would take him almost two on a bike. Dominique walks around the lot to see if anything has changed, and then he looks into the forest. Riyin walks up behind him with a jay-gun ready to shoot.

Riyin: What do you want here?

Dominique turns around, Riyin lowers his weapon, and they hug.

Riyin: It's good to have you back, we thought you were gone.

Dom: It got me but it didn't kill me. Where is the rest of the team?

Riyin: Back at the castle.

Dom: Call them back.

CHAPTER 12

THE PRIMARY OBJECTIVE

Now with Dominique back a wave of relief comes over the team as they sit in the lot meeting room.

Jade: Don't do anything like that again.

Dominique shakes his head.

Jamal: I bet it was a rush.

Dom: Crazy.

Jamal: You are going back?

Dom: I don't think so, it would be best for our plans. If I stay gone, I'm going to need a few things from my room.

They bring him back a box of disks. Dominique listens to the disk of the council meetings, finding out that they are going to leave Jade and Jamal alone since he's gone. Dominique gets up and goes outside to breathe some fresh air. A few feet away, Mustang walks around the forest stopping at the edge of the lot, and under the cover of the forest he sees the lot, the gun towers, and carts. He sees Dominique walking around the lot, as Mustang looks at Dominique, Riyin walks up behind him coming from hunting. Riyin sneaks up behind him and knocks Mustang out. Minutes later, Mustang wakes up in a cell with Dominique standing on the outside.

Mustang: I knew you weren't dead.

Dom: I'm not that easy to kill, what are you doing out this far?

Mustang: Just walking, it's my cycle of rest. You're planning something, aren't you?

Dominique walks away, Mustang gets up.

Mustang: I've just learned what happen to the vampires.

Dominique stops walking.

Mustang: They don't talk about it with us much, only that it was their greatest but easiest victory. After training with you, I can see that can't be true. I was born on a wolf ruled planet, With a hand full of my brother sin-tars, we were trained by a wolf named Victor along side other wolves and amazons, and then I was shipped here.

Dominique turns to Mustang.

Mustang: But I don't trust them. I want to be part of your plan.

Dom: Well, you are one of my best students, what can you tell me about the sin-tars and wolves here?

Mustang: From what I know, they were guns for hire. The only reason they joined the wolves was because the price was right. And the wolves, the only thing I know is that they are from Pluto, and it's still spinning.

Dominique lets Mustang out, and they go outside to talk.

Dom: This is dangerous water you're treading in. I'm only gonna say this once. This isn't just about revenge, it's about putting the planet back in the right hands, and if you betray me, you will suffer a fate more painful than the wolves. Am I understood?

Mustang: Yes sir.

They shake hands, and Mustang goes back into the forest, Dominique just keeps walking around. After a month of working in the forests lab continuing with Jade and Jamal's work, he creates a small army of twenty soldiers (ten men and ten women, all looking about nineteen years old). After a year of training and learning, he breaks them down into teams of five and puts one person at the lead of each team. The leader of team 1 is Sal, a male; team 2, Jake, a male; team 3, Trish, a female; and team 4, Palleen, a female. As the soldiers train, Dominique, and his team stand around talking.

Jamal: You think they're ready?

Dom: Not yet, I want their combat skills to compeat with ours.

Jade: It seems they don't have that far to go.

Dom: I know. (with a smile).

Later, Dominique, Jade, and Jamal work in the gun room. The alarms go off, they go outside with their guns out. As a small ship comes toward them and lands on the lot, the ship door opens and three vampires a few years older then the team walk out (two women and a man). One of the women starts to walk up.

Jamal: That must be their leader.

Dom: Where do you come from?

Woman: We are from the stars, among other places, but our mothers are from this planet. My name is La-dasha; this is Tallin and Varook. We are survivors of the war.

The team and the survivors go into the meeting room to talk.

La-dasha: Before the battles became a full out war, our pregnant mothers were sent to the stars to be safe then return when the time was right. But the time never became right. Our mothers died years ago, after that we trained ourselves along with getting ourselves in and out of various situation's. Now we are back to gain control, but I see that you have already done that.

Dom: We were created in a lab by the wolves not too far from here, we're what you call… living weapons. We know what they have done, and it will be delt with accordingly. We now hav under our control what they have been looking for, let's just say we have the blood of the seven deep within our veins.

La-dasha: The seven? My grandmother was master of the lightning element.

Dominique just smiles. The survivors get cleaned up, get some food and rest. Hours later, they meet Dominique and his team outside on the lot.

Dom: So you three had quite an adventure out there. I want to see what you got.

The survivors stand back to back surrounded by the team. Dominique cracks his knuckles before running at them, they move out of the way as Dominique moves in swinging, becoming surrounded by the survivors swinging at him. Dominique blocks some of the hits dodging the others, Tallin hits him on the mid-section, making him stumble back. They all run at Dominique, throwing punches, Dominique blocks but some connect, Dominique throws some back that connect. Dominique kicks Varook on the chest, making him stumble back, and then blocks a punch from Tallin hitting her on the side with his palm. She stumbles back, La-dasha hits

Dominique on the face, making him stumble to the side. Tallin and Varook run at Dominique, they kick and punch at him, he blocks but some connect. La-dasha runs at Dominique, Jade rushes La-dasha before she gets to Dominique, they fall to the ground and roll, Varook swings at Dominique, Dominique grabs his wrist and pulls him in the way of a jump kick from Tallin, making him fall and roll back. Jade sweep kicks La-dasha, La-dasha flips over Jade's leg and kicks at Jade before she can stand. Jade leans back and then swings at La-dasha as she stands up, La-dash-a jumps back. Tallin kicks at Dominique, Dominique grabs her foot and trips her. Dominique gets hit from the back on the side, making him stumble to the side. Tallin and Varook run at Dominique, they both swing and hit him on the chest. Dominique stumbles back and falls, rolling back to his feet. Riyin runs in, Jade and La-dasha swing at each other. Jade hits her on the neck and La-dasha hits her on the ribs. They both stumble to the side, Riyin kicks Varook on the side as he runs up making him stumble. Varook kicks Riyin back. Riyin blocks then hits him back making Varook fall back and roll. Riyin walks up to Varook, Varook swings and hits Riyin on the face and Riyin absorbs the hit then hits Varook back, lifting Varook off his feet ,landing on his back hard.

Dom: That will be all.

Everyone stops fighting, Jamal throws his hands up in disappointment before walking away.

Dom: You're good, with each others help we can all become better.

As they all rest up around the lot, La-dasha walks to the north end of the lot, bending on one knee, placing her hand on the sand. Dominique joins her.

Dom: So is Mars what you hoped it would be?

La-dasha: Not at all, I heard stories about how the planet was a big forest and now it is filled with the same dust I've seen my mother turned into when she died.

Dominique could hear the shadow king's voice and now knows what he meant when he told him the sands are filled with their bones. Dominique gets angry, his eyes start to fill up with tears, and then they start to glow. La-dasha just looks at Dominique.

Dom: This is the last day of hiding and not being seen. Night fall will be our homecoming. We will show them that the vampire name is something to fear once again. They will pay.

Nightfall Dominique walks up to his team at the edge of the east end of the forest. All the refugee kingdoms of Mars stand ready.

Dom: How are we doing?

Jamal: It's quiet right now, but it won't be for long.

Dom: Good, the repton war ships are on the way.

Dominique gets a call.

Reggie: Reggie to Dominique, we are ready to come in.

Dom: Good, stay put.

Dominique calls Mustang. Mustang walks around the kingdom control room looking around as he disconnects the alarms.

Dom: How's it going?

Mustang: It's all good. The systems are down, you can move now.

Dominique tells the ships to move in, the reptons slowly approach the kingdom but before anyone notice, the ships begin to fire on the kingdom. They spray the kingdom with bullets, knocking down homes and killing a lot of people. Troops come up behind the ships, killing anyone that was not dead or the ships missed. Dominique and Jade run into the castle, Jamal walks up to a wall and claps, bringing the wall down then makes his way to the kingdom lab, Dominique and Jade enter the castle meeting room and find the council in a meeting, the HC gets up and runs to a back room and locks the doors. Outside, Riyin and Mustang run into Strike and Katan.

Strike: Traitor!

Mustang: I'm just doing what my people do best. Go with the side that has the most to offer.

They run at each other. Inside, the HC stands in the back of the room he went into. All he hears is the rest of the council scream for their lives, then a knock on the doors, then an explosion send The doors go flying off the hinges, hitting the wall behind the HC, Dominique and Jade walk in.

HC: So you're not dead.

Dom: It shocked me too. And I think we found what you've been looking for.

Dominique lifts his hand to show the electricity coverings his hand.

HC: Now if you give them to me, you can go on with your lives.

Dom: I have a better idea; you and your people leave this planet.

HC: You want me gone? Remove me.

Dom: My pleasure.

Dominique runs at him, swings, and hits him on the face. The HC stumbles back, holding his nose. Dominique hits him on the chest, making him stumble back. Dominique goes to swings at him again; the HC kicks Dominique on the chest, lifting him off his feet with his back hitting the ground. Outside, Strike and Mustang run at each other. Strike flips over Mustang, landing on Mustang's back breaking one of his legs, and then jumps off, making him fall to the ground. Strike walks up to him lying on the ground and pulls his sword from his back. As he swings his sword, Riyin punches Strike from the side. Strike falls and rolls and then comes at Riyin. Riyin grabs Strike by the throat and slams him into the ground, and then hits Strike until his face is a bloody mess. Riyin stands up with blood dripping from his hands. Katan wakes up from getting knocked out, grabs a sword on the ground, and runs at Riyin from behind. She gets to him and then swings. Out of nowhere, a lightning bolt hits her killing her. Riyin looks back and sees La-dasha standing there with her hands up. Jamal runs down the hall of the kingdom lab, avoiding small fires and falling debris happening from explosions going off in the building, reaching a firearms room, as he enters Jamal and the HS cross paths, stopping both of the in their tracks. Back inside the castle, Dominique, Jade, and the HC are in a standoff, breathing hard.

HC: I'm done playing with you.

Then he starts to howl. Dominique cringes from the noise. The HC's hair begins to grow thicker all over his body, as he grows in size, his nose grows longer, his teeth and nails become very sharp, making him look like a monster wolf. They just look at him.

HC: You like what you see?

Dom: So you show us your real face, it's ugly, suits you.

HC: Not too many wolves can show this form. They say when you come of age, you can't do this anymore, but I still can.

The HC runs at them swinging; they move out the way, Jade pulls out her bo staff. The HC howls; they cover their ears. Dominique runs at the HC and swings and hits him on the side. The HC doesn't move. The HC swings and hits Dominique, making him stumble back. Jade runs up and hits the HC on the snout with her staff. The HC swings and cuts Jade's arm deep, making her fall down. As he swings at Jade again, Dominique drop-kicks him on the side, making him stumble. Dominique runs up again and gets backhanded. The hit sends him flying to the top of the wall getting stuck, and then he falls to the ground, hitting his head, breaking his rib cage and leg. Dominique looks around, but everything is blurry. At the lab they Looking at each other, Jamal stand paused as the HS uncontrollably quivers in fear. Suddenly the HS grabs a large gun, points it at Jamal and without hesitation fires, Jamal manages to clap seconds before the bullet leaves the camber sending a wave that forces the bullet go off inside the gun, making the gun explode in the HS's hands. The HS drops to his knees screaming holding what use to be his hands, Jamal walks up to the HS pull out his sidearm and shoot the HS at point blank range in the head. As he tries to regain his vision, the HC sees Dominique out of it and runs at him at full speed on all fours. Dominique fills the HC running toward him. Dominique pulls out his Doom knife and puts the end of the knife handle in the palm of his hand with his power making it stick. As the HC gets to Dominique, Dominique puts out his hand. As the HC sinks his teeth into Dominic's flesh reaching bone about to bite off Dominique's arm, Dominique shoots the doom knife from his hand into the HC's mouth. The knife busts out the back of his head, along with brains, pieces of skull and sparks. The knife goes flying across the room sticking in a wall before the HC's body hit the ground dead. Dominique just sits there looking at the body. He gets up and helps Jade. Before they walk out the room, Dominique reaches back; retrieving the doom knife. They go outside to see that everyone in the Mars kingdom was dead and a kingdom in ruins, and the vampires are putting the dead bodies into large fires. Dominique sits down on the castle steps. Tri-sarh walks up to Dominique. He stands up. A vampire comes out of the castle and hands him a case, and Dominique gives her the case.

Dom: It's all in there.

Tri-sarh: It's good doing business with you. Let us know if you ever need us again.

Dom: Will do.

They shake hands, and the reptons leave Mars. Dominique walks around the kingdom looking at the mess and then up at the moon. He thinks about what the HC said knowing it is far from over and they are in for something big. So with that, he starts to make plans in his head to prepare and rebuild as they wait for what's to come next.

www.ingramcontent.com/pod-product-compliance
Lightning Source LLC
LaVergne TN
LVHW041609070526
838199LV00052B/3049